THE GREAT RUSH

"Where's the posse, Sheriff?" Ayers asked.

Into the little intervening silence came the unmistakable beat of many ridden horses coming into Alturas from the northeast, all in a rushing body.

Ayers turned, stepped to the door, craned northward, remained motionless for a long second, then sighed and stepped back. "I reckon we won't need a posse," he told Lew. "That's Eagleton and his crew. They're heading this way and they're armed to the ears."

Halfmoon Ranch

LAURAN PAINE

LEISURE BOOKS NEW YORK CITY

A LEISURE BOOK®

April 2010

Published by special arrangement with Golden West Literary Agency.

Dorchester Publishing Co., Inc.
200 Madison Avenue
New York, NY 10016

ISBN 10: 0-8439-6342-5
ISBN 13: 978-0-8439-6342-7
E-ISBN: 978-1-4285-0845-3

The name "Leisure Books" and the stylized "L" with design are trademarks of Dorchester Publishing Co., Inc.

Printed in the United States of America.

10 9 8 7 6 5 4 3 2 1

Visit us online at www.dorchesterpub.com.

Table of Contents

Ocean of Grass

I

The skin above Slim Liskey's eyes was drawn back in a deep frown, and his pale blue eyes were hard. Below, in the great Grass Valley a crew of cowboys was moving a large herd of fat cattle; feed was gone now and the chill of early autumn was in the air. Grass Valley was where the Liskeys had fall fed their cattle for two generations. He always rode up in the late summer, just before he brought the cattle in, but today, for the first time in his memory—and the memory of the old-timers, too, for that matter— some other cow outfit had dared to take over.

Slim sat in angry silence on the skyline. He couldn't make out who the trespassers were, and he had no intention of riding down to find out. It was too late to go back to the Circle L for riders. The men below would have their cattle halfway to wherever they were going to take them before he could get help and come back. Besides, while the anger within him demanded vengeance, he saw that the feed was gone—eaten down to bare ground. That was what counted, the fall feed.

He watched the riders line out their herd, and his jaw muscles rippled. The grass was gone; Circle L cattle would have to be hay fed earlier—which meant considerable extra expense. The Circle L was in the cow business to make money, and, while they could afford a few extra tons of feed, it still didn't sit well— especially with falling beef prices and a poor calf crop.

The lowing of the cattle as they left the ocean of grass behind came faintly, insistently to the lone rider. Now and then he heard profanity, or the herding yell of a rider. A small dust cloud rose around men and animals, and Slim begrudgingly admired the scene. Born and raised a cattleman, he loved the activity below him. It was part and parcel of himself. Any other time, any other place, Liskey would have been just another man—perhaps a menial one at that, but here in his own environment he was a symbol of the cowmen. He was the heir of the old-timers who had swept across the Great Plains and mountain ranges with the bawling herds, restlessly searching for the perfect cattle country—fighting, drinking, swearing, and sweating themselves into early graves, slaves to their trade.

Slim reined his horse around and started back down the twisting deer trail he had ridden up to the horizon. His mind was busy; he would get a fresh horse and head for town. Liskey frowned; it was odd that he hadn't heard about these trespassing cowmen in Grass Valley from the other ranchers and riders in the country. Strange, too, that those men would just barge in and take over land that had been Liskey free range for generations. Slim shrugged. The die was cast and the feed gone, that was certain. He'd have to start winter feeding a couple of months early. He rolled a cigarette grimly. But next year there would be no cattle in Grass Valley unless they wore the brand of the Circle L!

"Goin' to eat, Slim?"

Slim looked up absently from where he was slapping a dry saddle blanket under his scarred saddle near the gray old corrals. "I reckon." There wasn't any enthusiasm in the halfhearted answer. In fact, his preoccupation had robbed him of his appetite.

"Then git in here."

Slim looked up quickly from the left side of the fresh horse he was saddling. Normally his brother's abrupt way didn't bother him, but this evening it did. He opened his mouth to reply, hesitated for a long second, then clamped his jaws shut.

Inside the old house, bravely trying to look fresh under many harsh winters and several coats of indifferent and inexpensive paint, Slim washed himself methodically, ran a comb through his short chestnut hair, and dropped into a battered chair next to the kitchen table.

Slim's brother was older—raw-boned, ham-handed, and gray-headed. There was a strong family resemblance in the jaw and the pale blue eyes, but where Slim was little and well-proportioned, Buff was taciturn, thin-lipped, and rangy. His age was evident in the heavy, sagging lines around his mouth and eyes. It was obvious from the way he treated his younger brother that he had practically raised him. "What in hell kept you so long over in Grass Valley?"

Slim ate several mouthfuls of tender steak before he answered. "There was a bunch of riders driving a herd out of the grass."

For a long moment Buff stared at his brother. It was inconceivable to him that anyone would dare to take Liskey grass. His nostrils distended dangerously while he waited for the younger man to continue. Slim swallowed some coffee.

"Didn't get close enough to see who they were, but their cattle have been in the grass for quite a spell.

Anyway, the fall feed's gone." There was a finality to the last sentence that told Buff all he had to know.

The elder Liskey's eyes flashed fire. "Tomorrow take Sam an' Caleb an' hunt up them fellers. By Gawd, no one will rob us like that an' git away with it."

Slim looked at his brother and chewed his supper calmly. Buff knew that what he had said was foolish when he said it—but his anger demanded release.

"Reckon I'll ride in to Searchlight tonight an' ask a few questions." Slim's remark was gently made, Buff nodded in agreement, and turned back to the cook stove, as two sweat-stained riders trooped up to the house from the corral.

Sam and Caleb Masters were brothers. They were sturdily built, taciturn, and unimaginative men. Their people had been in the country since time out of mind and had left them a legacy of laziness, slow minds, quick tempers—and nothing else. They had been cowboying for the Liskeys for three years— mainly because the food was plentiful and, except for calving time and winter feeding, the work wasn't very hard. With somber nods both Sam and Caleb ducked their heads to Buff and Slim, washed noisily, and sat down at the oilcloth-covered table.

Slim groomed himself a little more than usual; he put on a clean shirt under his Levi jumper, grunted to the three men still eating, and went out into the night. The ride to Searchlight was commonplace. Slim's eyes noticed the brittle tingle to the starlight and his thoughts automatically turned to the likelihood of an early frost this year. He swung easily to the mile-eating walk of his horse and didn't evidence anything but instinct until he was riding into the north end of Searchlight's wide, dusty, and only main thoroughfare.

Searchlight was loud with nightly revelry. Slim was mildly surprised to see so many horses at the hitch rails, and hear so much noise; normally a weekday night in town was comparatively quiet. He rode up to the massive and smooth old log rail in front of Townley's Emporium, swung off, and tied up, casually noticing that all of the business establishments in town were dark. Next to Townley's was the Horseshoe Saloon; orange-yellow light from its many lamps was casting uncertain and warm shadows onto the plank sidewalk.

In the Horseshoe was a familiar atmosphere. The heat of glowing bodies, hissing lamps, and hazy tobacco smoke kept the chill of the autumn night outside. Slim grinned at several men who nodded to him. He walked methodically up to the bar and eased in beside old Harry Rowell—who owned the Horseshoe—and a tall, lean stranger who had Texan written all over him.

Rowell was short with a high paunch, flamboyant boots, and a great silver and gold belt buckle, too big for his size and girth. He was a genial man with restless eyes and a generous, slack-looking mouth. "Buy you a drink, Slim?"

Slim smiled easily. He knew Harry well—had known him all of his life and, despite the things he had heard, liked the man. Old Rowell was a great practical joker, on occasion.

"Yeah, reckon you can give me a shot of the best whiskey you've got in the house."

Rowell grinned widely and motioned to the dour-faced bartender. Slim drank the smooth whiskey and felt his body relax. He turned slowly toward Rowell. "Harry, you know about 'most everything that goes on around here. Tell me somethin'. Who had their cattle in Grass Valley this summer?"

Rowell's face was screwed up for an instant, then a look of caution went over his features. "Well, hell, Slim, might be anybody."

Slim shook his head lazily and his eyes were speculative. "No, you know better than that. Grass Valley has been Liskey grazing for more years than you an' I can count together. The local cowmen wouldn't touch it . . . any more than we'd trespass on their fall feedin' grounds. You know that."

Rowell shrugged as though he was getting tired of the conversation.

"Damned if I know, Slim, but, after all, that grass don't *belong* to you folks. It's open land, y'know, an' actually anybody can go in there."

Slim raised his eyebrows slightly. "Well, in a way you're right enough, but in another way you're wrong, too. Us Liskeys have been grazin' up there since my grandpa's day an' that gives us range rights."

Rowell smiled easily; he wasn't to be baited into anything. "Sure . . . we all know that. Slim, but maybe there's strangers that don't." Rowell turned away with evident relief when someone hailed him from across the room. Slim recognized the exaggerated way he moved away for what it was—an opportunity to ease out of a conversation that was becoming distasteful to him. He watched Rowell's broad back with mild interest, then turned back to the bar.

Slim was into his second drink when the lean Texan beside him, pretty well liquored up, turned slowly and faced him. "What's the matter, sonny . . . lose some winter feed?"

Slim's gorge rose a trifle at the sound in the man's voice. "If you aren't a native from hereabouts, I wouldn't worry about it."

The Texan smiled. His teeth were large and even beneath a slightly hooked nose and squinted dark eyes. "Oh, hell, lad . . . I'm not the worryin' kind, none at all. It's just that I hate to see you little fellers git hurt." There was definite insult in the voice this time.

Slim turned with slitted eyes. "Speakin' of gettin' hurt, mister, it might just happen to you if you don't mind your own damned business."

The Texan looked mildly surprised and his black eyes swept over Liskey. The voice was quietly deliberate. "Mebbe so, junior, but I don't reckon it'll be by you."

II

Possibly—under normal circumstances—there would have been no violence, but both men were flooded with liquor-inspired belligerency. Slim's boot snaked out and around the Texan's foot; at the same time, his hand pushed firmly against the stranger's chest. The Texan went over backward with a startled oath. Slim watched him fall with detached interest. For a second the Texan eyed the rancher in the stillness of the barroom; his face was suffused with red, his eyes wide in concentrated fury.

From out of nowhere, Harry Rowell planted his ridiculous figure between the men and faced the Texan. His voice was quiet but his words carried. "No trouble in here, stranger. If you want to make war, go outside."

The saloon owner's words seemed puny in the face of the Texan's anger, but the dead silence of the crowded large room gave them a sound of authority that made the Texan drop his hand from his holstered .45 as he arose and dusted himself off.

Slim Liskey's irritation passed as quickly as it had come. He turned to the sullen Texan. "Have a drink?" There was neither challenge nor fear in the words and the stranger eyed him for a long moment before he edged up to the bar, his eyes quizzically unpleasant. "All right."

For a half an hour the two men stood side-by-side and drank. Slim was morose. He thought about the feed that was gone, but that wasn't really the cause of his mood because—while a little extra work and additional expense was involved—the Liskey brothers had run up against worse obstacles than this since they had inherited the ranch, five years ago.

It must have been the unaccustomed drinking that caused the sensation, at any rate; he turned to his silent companion. "Aren't you a Texan?"

The dark-eyed man nodded solemnly. "Yup."

Slim's face screwed into a questioning look. "Huntin' work?"

The Texan shook his head scornfully. "Nope."

Exasperated, Slim asked the stranger just what in hell he was doing in the Searchlight country, anyway.

The Texan drew himself up to his full six feet and better and glared down at the shorter man. "Damned if you ain't the nosiest feller I ever met." Having delivered himself of that opinion, he let the haughty look slide from his face, and he reached for the dark oak-colored bottle on the bar before them. "As a matter of fac' I've just finished workin' fer a feller named Whiting. Fred Whiting."

He nodded gravely as he poured a drink for himself and one for Slim. "This here Whiting's not a bad feller. He buys cattle on borrowed money, leases land, an' runs the cattle on the land. S'posed to make money at it, but, just between us, he'll never make money at cattle 'cause he's no cattleman." Having allowed this philosophical jewel to tumble from his thickening tongue, the Texan downed his drink, shuddered until even the gun in its worn holster on his hip vibrated alarmingly, then fell silent, moodily watching the whiskey bottle.

Slim digested what the stranger had told him as

he downed his own drink; he made a wry face and rapidly rolled a cigarette and popped it into his mouth. "S'funny, I was born an' raised in this country an' I've never heard of this feller, Whiting." He shook his head, which was beginning to accumulate a roseate fuzz around its inner workings.

The Texan grunted and scratched his hooked nose. "Don't feel bad. I never knew him, either, until I went to work for him." Confident that he had appeased young Liskey's sufferings somewhat, the Texan smiled in a fatherly fashion. "We jus' brought some cattle in off a real nice grass range north of town an' they ought to bring a good price. They was as fat as butterballs."

Something in the back of Slim's mind nudged him. "Where was all this grass?"

The Texan shrugged casually. "North of town, I told ya. Hell, I'm a Texan, an' I don't know nothin' about this New Mexico country at all." He raised his voice when he mentioned his home state and sarcasm dripped from his lips when he mentioned New Mexico.

Slim let the intended insult pass. "Well, all right, Tex, but what did this here grass country look like?"

Tex shrugged again indifferently. "Oh, it was a kind of a valley, but big as hell an' stirrup deep in grass."

The fumes in Liskey's brain struggled and finally overpowered the warning signal that told him the Texan was talking about Grass Valley. "Big Grass Valley, huh?"

The Texan nodded lugubriously and ran his tongue over his chapped lips.

Slim shook his head in a downward, lowering

fashion and from somewhere within him came a recurrence of his anger of several hours before. Grass Valley. Whiting. Winter feed. He turned slightly out-of-focus eyes on his companion. "Dammit. I believe you're one of the fellers who was driving cattle out of Grass Valley today."

The Texan nodded uncomprehendingly. "Yup." He nodded softly. "I sure helped drive Whiting's cows today, an' they was in a grass valley, too." Instinctively he turned—just in time to see Slim's hand coming up. He stepped backward and wagged a tanned finger. "No you don't. Damned if I ever seen such a country. Everybody wants to push a man down." There was a plaintive, almost pleading tone to his voice. "Hell, ain't you fellers ever heard of guns?"

Slim stared unsteadily. "Sure." He was reaching for his Colt when a claw-like hand grabbed him roughly by the shoulder and swung him around. Being completely unprepared for the rear assault, Slim tried to keep his balance, lurched uncertainly, and fell soddenly. There was disgust in the voice that came eerily to him as he floated gently out of earshot.

"I wouldn't've believed it. Slim Liskey, drunker'n a skunk. Why I ought to rawhide his bottom and send him home to Buff. Dammit, I think I'll just lock him up for the night." There was a hush before the nasal voice continued complainingly. "Yeah, an' we'll just toss this hard-looking playmate of his in, too. Take their guns boys. Thanks, Harry, fer the tip about trouble brewin' in your place." The voice trailed off as the sheriff and his deputies lugged the two cowboys away. "Why I've knowed that young scalawag since he was in short pants, an' him drunker'n a hooty owl." A few choice words of colorful and blistering profanity completed the tirade.

Searchlight, New Mexico was on a high plateau and the sun burst upon it every morning with a blinding splash of brilliant light. Normally Slim Liskey enjoyed the clear prismatic splendor that came up over the rugged land, but the morning after his disastrous sojourn in the Horseshoe Saloon he winced in spite of himself when he opened his eyes. The sun was only partly responsible, at that, because he recognized his abode as one of the three, whitewashed cells in Sheriff Carter's jailhouse. Lying prone on his pallet, he heard muted voices coming through the partition from the office. One voice was unmistakably old Carter's and then the sheriff identified the other as Fred Whiting, the cattle operator who had appropriated Grass Valley.

"Well . . . now look, Whiting," the sheriff's high-pitched voice came through the flimsy wall, "outsiders are welcome here in Searchlight as long as they behave themselves. But we don't stand fer no trouble, an' that goes fer Texans as well as anybody else. As a matter of fact, in my opinion, Texans ain't very. . . ."

The speaker was interrupted by a low, smooth voice that held a tinge of impatience in it. "All right, Sheriff, I know how you feel. After all the man doesn't even work for me any more. I'm just trying to get him out of your hair."

Whiting realized his error too late. The sheriff was bald, and his face colored deeply as he ran his hand self-consciously over his shiny dome. "Damned if I have to take your lip, Whiting. I've a notion to toss you in, too. I still have an empty cell."

Whiting protested vehemently. "I'm sorry, Sheriff. I didn't mean anything personal at all. Only I'll go Tex's bail an' get him out of the country if you'll turn him loose."

The sheriff pulled his shapeless old black Stetson over his shiny cranium with a vicious tug. He sat for a moment in deep silence, apparently thinking over Whiting's offer. Finally he nodded shortly. "All right. Reckon he's your man an' you can have him. For a price."

"How much?"

"Uh, make it twenty-five dollars."

Whiting hesitated and his color heightened. He opened his mouth to protest and Sheriff Carter's jaw settled into its usual uncompromising position. Whiting sighed audibly and swore under his breath as he unrolled a wad of bills and counted out the bail. He was irritated at Tex, the sheriff, and at himself as well. He had taken his cattle out of the country only to discover that he was short several head and now he had to re-hire his former riders in order to go back and hunt strays.

Sheriff Carter counted the crumpled bills with much finger licking, arose, and grabbed up a ring of keys. "Jest set an' relax. I'll go get your man." As he went through the door, he said, more to himself than to anyone else: "He's learned his lesson by now, so I'd jest as well turn young Liskey loose, too."

Slim was on his feet and waiting when Sheriff Carter released him. He nodded shortly into Carter's accusing eyes and edged his way into the office. Tex had already been released and was standing uncomfortably near Carter's battered desk. Whiting was tilted back against the wall in a round-back chair. His eyes were cold and intent as he looked at Tex.

"Get your gear Tex, an' let's get going." There was a commanding, threatening timbre to the man's words and the Texan flushed but said nothing.

Sheriff Carter grumpily rummaged in his desk and brought out two limp cartridge belts with sagging .45s dangling from them. Slim buckled his belt on slowly, facing the cattleman, Whiting.

"Understand you run a lot of cattle, Whiting."

The cowman's eyes flickered appraisingly over the young rancher. "Yes." The single word carried a multitude of meaning. It meant—"Mind your own business."—"What's it to you?"—and "Don't bother me, sonny."—all in one breath. Slim was stung to quick anger.

"Well, I'm going to pass something on to you. When you're in a new country, find out where you can run your stock, an' where you can't."

Whiting came up out of the chair in a well co-ordinated movement. "Just what in hell are you driving at, cowboy?"

Liskey took two steps forward and checked himself as he felt the sheriff's critical eye on him. "You ran a herd of cattle in Grass Valley, Whiting, an' that's feed that's been used by my family for two generations. No one hereabouts would pull a stunt like that, but then I reckon you didn't know Grass Valley was closed territory. That's what I mean when I say find out where you can run stock in a new country."

Whiting grinned easily but his eyes were cold and unfriendly. "I'll run cattle anywhere I damned well please, cowboy, as long as the land ain't deeded . . . understand?"

Slim's anger was almost beyond his ability to control. "Listen, Whiting, if you ever so much as step your foot onto our range again, I'll personally run you out of the country."

Whiting shrugged caustically. "Go get your runnin' clothes on, cowboy, because I'm goin' back up to your precious range today and hunt for strays. I'm short five thousand dollars' worth of cattle, an' I aim to get 'em."

Liskey doubled up his fist as Whiting turned to Sheriff Carter. Slim saw the sheriff eyeing his fist with an approving but deprecating stare.

"Sheriff, you heard this man threaten me, an' I'm here to tell you that I'll hold you personally responsible if anyone interferes with my men hunting for strays today."

The sheriff mulled over what the cowman had said as Whiting headed for the door with his Texan cowboy in tow.

"I'll be damned if you do."

But the door was closing on Whiting as Sheriff Carter answered. He regarded the closed door doubtfully, then turned jaundiced eyes on Slim. "Why in hell do you have to get into hot water an' stay in it? Bad enough to get drunk, but now you've even got me in trouble." He sighed mightily and motioned with a weary arm toward the door. "Get to hell out of here, will you, please?"

III

Slim mulled over the happenings of the evening before as he rode back toward the Circle L. He knew what would happen if he told Buff of the Whiting incident, and, while he recognized the advantages of direct action, he also knew his brother well enough to realize that Buff's reaction would be both explosive and violent beyond the bounds of control. He grudgingly decided to say nothing to Buff about Grass Valley or Whiting—after all, the feed was gone.

When Slim rode into the Circle L yard, the morning sun was beginning to get warm. He dismounted and unsaddled his horse just as Buff came out of the blacksmith shed.

"Where in hell have you been?"

Slim finished unsaddling, turned his horse loose, and regarded his fiery brother with a calm and somewhat bloodshot eye. "Got smoked up a little at Rowell's place an' spent the night in the lock-up."

Buff looked his surprise as his brother headed for the house. Nearby, two riders silently exchanged a quick look and a glint of amusement showed in their eyes. Buff was a known hell-raiser, but Slim had always been the quiet, calm, and thoughtful member of the family.

As the riders swung aboard their horses and headed out, and Buff walked slowly toward the house after his brother, a hasty and somewhat stormy council was in progress back in the Horseshoe Saloon at Searchlight.

Behind a cluttered oaken table that served as a desk, Harry Rowell faced Fred Whiting. He was shaking his head as he spoke.

"I told you when you went in there, Fred, that the Liskeys an' their riders might not stumble onto you until fall. They damned seldom ride to Grass Valley until just before they push their cattle in." He shrugged. "You knew the chance you were takin' an' personally I think you're a damned fool if you insist on goin' back after the few strays that may be up there. After all, you've made plenty on the weight gain of them cattle. What few more dollars you'll take out ain't worth the risk of gettin' shot over."

Fred Whiting chewed slowly on a long, thin panatela that was unlighted. "You may be right, Harry, but a man hates to lose money he's got made."

Rowell leaned back and his large, slack features were blanketed with disgust. "Suit yourself, Fred. I've got my cut out of steering you onto the land. But if you're smart, you'll let well enough alone. The graveyards are full of fellers who went back after that last buck." Rowell stood up. His attitude clearly signified that the conversation was over. Whiting arose, also, and looked speculatively at Rowell. There was a moment's silence, then Rowell frowned slightly.

"Well?"

Whiting clamped his jaw on the cigar. "I'm goin' after 'em."

Rowell moved brusquely toward the door without a word, opened it, and held it open until Whiting passed through into the noisy saloon proper. Rowell's bearing made it very clear that he had washed his hands of the entire affair. Without a word Fred Whiting nodded to three cowboys lounging at the bar and walked out of the saloon. The riders followed their boss and Rowell's small eyes were edged in contempt as he watched the quartet leave.

Outside the Horseshoe, Fred Whiting's orders were explicit. "Get mounted, boys, an' head for Grass Valley. I'll get my horse from the livery barn an' join you on the trail. We've got cattle to find today." His eyes narrowed a trifle. "Some local cowmen may be up there soon tryin' to make trouble for us"—he shrugged eloquently—"but then I reckon you Texans can handle anything that comes up."

The riders were all hard-eyed, lean men; they smiled meaningly. All, that is, but the one who had been thrown in jail with young Liskey. He studied the toes of his boots and said nothing. Whiting nodded briefly and headed for the livery barn.

The Texans strode easily to Rowell's hitch rack, untied, and swung aboard. A youngish man with sandy hair and a badly healed nose that had once been broken, turned to the one-time drinking partner of Slim Liskey. "I thought you got paid off yesterday."

Tex nodded. "I did, then I got dumped in the *calabozo* an' Whiting bailed me out . . . so I gotta help you guys the balance of the week to square up fer the bail money."

The cowboys laughed raucously, and, as their horses loped along smoothly on the dusty road out of Searchlight, Tex was the ungrateful recipient of some blunt jokes.

Grass Valley actually was open range, but after the time-honored precedent of common usage the Liskey family held control of it. This arrangement was weak and awkward at best, but nevertheless the law of the range at that time. Whiting's hirelings loped easily along until they came to the cut-off that headed by a circuitous and tree-shaded trail into the heart of the vast ocean of grass that was their destination. As fate would have it, the Liskey hired hands were returning to the home ranch along a narrow, craggy old hog-back when Whiting's Texans jumped their first stray, a slab-sided old cow with wild eyes and wickedly curved horns that had been dubbed. There was a well-marked, fat youngster by her side. The Texans whooped at sight of the boomer and headed her for the low land near the trail, where they could pick her up later.

Caleb Masters turned to his pinch-faced brother. "Don't know who them fellers is, but they got no call to chase cattle in Grass Valley. Let's go 'vestigate."

Sam Masters had the wide shoulders and narrow hips of a powerful man. His features were narrow and not as generously rounded as those of his brother, and, although his eyes held little more than a hint of animal intelligence, he shook his head wisely. "Nope. I ain't goin' down there. They's three of 'em. Besides . . . fer all we know . . . that critter may be a stray an' belong to 'em."

Caleb was silent as he watched the Texans haze the wild boomer down to lower feed. He shrugged sulkily. "Well, then, if we ain't goin' down, let's get on back to the ranch. It's close to eatin' time." He shook out his reins, and the two men rode slowly, leisurely on to the corrals of the Circle L.

Caleb and Sam were close by when Buff bellowed the noon meal. They entered the massive old kitchen with exaggerated unconcern, washed methodically, and lit into the food. The meal was a quiet one. Slim ate across from Buff, who was the only man on the ranch who could cook. Buff chewed with the short, incisive bites of an impatient man.

Seated, ready to enjoy his lumpy hand-rolled cigarette and black coffee, Sam Masters lighted up. " 'Seen three riders chasin' a wild cow an' a calf in Grass Valley this morning."

There was an abrupt cessation to the air of mealtime harmony. Slim looked hastily, furtively at Buff while the latter was staring at Sam, a jowl full of partially masticated food held in a state of suspension. "Who were they?"

Sam shrugged indifferently, too stolid to sense the suddenly charged atmosphere at the table. Buff chewed and swallowed with definite finality. "Who's critter was they chasin'?"

Sam shrugged again and Slim headed off the explosion he saw building up in his older brother's face. "When I was in . . . ah . . . town last night, I run onto the feller who run cattle in the valley." Buff's eyes were wrathfully accusing but Slim ignored the look and hurried on with his conversation. "Name's Whiting . . . Fred Whiting. I don't know much about him except that he's got a crew of three or four Texans ridin' for him, an' they're goin' out today an' hunt for strays that they figured might still be in Grass Valley."

Buff got up from the table and his face wasn't pleasant. "Damn you fellers anyway. I'm tryin' to build this ranch up. That means conservin' our feed, an' you bunch of backsliders aren't doin' a damned thing to help me." His mouth was open to say more when Slim came up out of his chair reluctantly.

"Listen, Buff"—the voice was quiet and even—"you got no more to say around here than I have."

Buff slashed the air with a balled-up fist. "What's that got to do with it?"

"Just this." Slim's eyes were dark with anger and his jaw was squared against the pressure of his clenched teeth. "This here Whiting's used up our food. It's gone. We'll have to fall feed early this year." He shrugged and some of the fury went out of his face. "All right. We've been robbed this year, an' there's no gettin' around it, but if you start a fight, an' maybe somebody gets killed, we'll be in a worse shape than we're in now . . . an' we still won't have any fall feed." He shrugged again. "So let's let it go by this time an' keep a better watch on Grass Valley next year. After all, feudin' won't give us an extra shock of hay."

Buff's face was harsh and Slim's hopes of averting trouble faded as he watched his brother. Buff turned away with a muttered word of profane scorn. "Well, how about it, Sam an' Caleb? You goin' to sit on your tails while Circle L feed is stole right out from under us . . . or are you goin' up to Grass Valley with me an' put a stop to this here trespassin' once an' for all?"

For several long seconds no one moved in the Circle L kitchen and the even, imperturbable *ticktock* of the old Seth Thomas clock on the back wall sounded as loudly as a hammer on an anvil. Finally Sam Masters got up, picked his hat off the floor by the side of his chair, hitched his sweat- and brushstained cartridge belt around his flat middle, and looked with cold, hard blue eyes at Buff. "When do we start?"

The words were a signal. Buff's face wreathed into a bleak smile and he turned to Slim, but the younger brother was avoiding the look of triumph he knew was meant for him.

Buff ignored Slim as the four men saddled fresh horses in efficient silence, swung aboard after checking side arms, and headed out of the yard in a spray of flying grit and madly gyrating spirals of dust. Slim's hangover, coupled with the leaden feeling in the pit of his stomach over the Grass Valley feed, made him a miserable ally. He rode along with the hope that he could avert what he feared might happen. It was useless to explain to Buff that Whiting had warned the sheriff that there might be trouble. When Buff Liskey was in a fighting mood, nothing mattered, come hell or high water, and one look at the elder Liskey's aquiline features was enough to convince the greenest pilgrim that war rode in the vanguard of the Circle L.

IV

Whiting had caught up with his men in Grass Valley; they had pushed four calving cows to the lower expanses of the valley when one of the Texans jerked his horse to a sliding halt that made churned-up earth erupt into a miniature cyclone. The cowboy was staring hard back down the trail and his profile was a study in uneasy alertness. Fred Whiting saw the rider stop and looked up quizzically. He followed the direction of his rider's stare and swore abruptly and harshly into the clear air.

With a shout that reflected both a warning and a caution, Fred Whiting motioned to his riders to converge on him. By this time the Whiting cowboys had seen the hard-riding Circle L coming across the valley in a dead run, and spurred toward their employer out of the dual desire to be on hand for the fireworks and to obtain the strength of numbers.

Unthinkingly Fred Whiting had made himself the point of juncture for both sides and saw his mistake too late. The Texans thundered up on their lathered horses, just as Buff and Slim Liskey with Caleb and Sam Masters roared to a sliding halt in front of Whiting's nervously side-stepping bay mare.

Buff's face was flushed and shiny with sweat. "Which of you is Whiting?"

There were no preliminaries and Whiting was no fool. He saw death squarely in front of him, as surely as he sat his horse. "What difference does it make?"

The answer was a stall but Buff had been through this sort of thing many times before. He shook his head savagely. "Cut it out, feller, or I'll chop you down without knowin' who you are."

"All right, cowboy, I'm Whiting, now . . . what's on your mind?"

Slim edged his horse forward so as to be offset between his brother and the trespassing cowman. Whiting's Texans were sitting like wooden statues, eyes beady and unblinking as they watched the Masters boys and Slim. Caleb and Sam had the peculiar animal courage that would face death with perfect calm, because imagination had been left out of their intellectual make-up.

Buff was sitting tall and slightly forward in the saddle. "Well, Whiting, you got a choice here in Grass Valley, either you pay us for the feed you stole, or go fer your gun."

Whiting licked his lips with the tip of his tongue and Slim felt a twinge of contempt for the man. Whiting had been as hard as nails in Sheriff Carter's office that morning, but now it was different. Then Slim got a surprise. Whiting gave Buff stare for stare.

"You must be Liskey." He nodded sideways without taking his eyes from Buff's face. "I recognized your brother when you rode up." Buff's eyes flashed and he opened his mouth to speak when Whiting continued in a calm voice. "This here valley don't belong to you, Liskey. It's open range, an' anybody can use it." He nodded casually to emphasize his point. "Sure . . . you've had the use of it for a long time, but it still isn't yours, so I'm not going to pay you a damned dime for the grass my critters ate here"—he lowered his voice a little—"an' I'm not going for my gun, either."

Buff's face was contorted and twitching with white-hot anger. Slim recognized the signs, and, while he wanted in the worst way to control what he knew was going to happen, his better judgment told him now was no time to ride between the men—or for that matter to take his eyes off of the Texans.

Buff suddenly sank his *Californio* spurs into his leggy grullo gelding and the startled animal leaped like a deer right up beside Whiting's mare. Something swished and whined through the air like a streak of gray lightning and Buff's shot-loaded quirt described a vicious arc and struck the cowman an angling blow across the cheek bone, chin, and throat. Whiting was taken completely by surprise and the force of the blow unhorsed him. He rolled frantically, blunderingly in a state of semi-consciousness away from the wildly moving horses legs above him as the Texans went into action.

Borrowing a tactic from the Comanche cavalry of their native state, the Texans fanned out in a rough circle around the Circle L riders in a spinning and spurring blur of movement. Guns flashed dully in the early afternoon sun and the first volley caught Sam Masters's horse dead center. The animal went down with a graceful, gentle collapse that left the rider standing across the still body, gun blazing with the accuracy never achieved on a running or frightened horse. Caleb and Slim were struck with the same idea at the same time; both slid from their horses, darted over to Sam's dead mount, and flung themselves down behind the warm, sweaty carcass. The Texans were out of pistol range by this time and the Circle L faction had no opportunity to make their shots count.

Buff hobbled up to his brother and flopped down

beside him. "Damned bushwhackers got me in the back of the leg."

Slim looked backward and down with a critical gaze. The wound was a deep cut, nothing more, but Slim would have felt no sympathy if it had been a bad one. Buff was a fool—a hotheaded, belligerent fool. Here they were in a fine position to get killed—and for what? The damned grass that was already gone—all the bullets and bloodshed in the world wouldn't bring it back until spring. He said nothing and squinted his eyes toward the Texans.

Fred Whiting was off to the left of the Circle L faction, kneeling on one leg shaking his head slowly back and forth like a wounded bear. Buff turned his head and watched the downed man. Whiting pushed himself slowly to his feet and looked dazedly around him. He saw his riders sitting their horses in a little huddle, out of bullet range for a handgun. Slowly, painfully he turned and looked vacantly at the Circle L men. The silence that had been so abruptly shattered a few minutes before had closed in again, each side watching the groggy cowman who stood alone a little behind and off to one side of the fighters.

Slim studied Whiting doubtfully. "He's hurt. No fight in him."

Buff swore flatly. "I'll dig some fight out of him."

Slim turned, but not quickly enough. Buff was on his feet, hobbling toward the lone enemy. Slim called out for his brother to come back, but Buff ignored the plea. Buff was almost in front of Whiting when one of the Texans raised his .45 slowly, aimed with almost rigid effort and meticulous care, and squeezed the trigger. Simultaneously with the pistol shot, a rifle *cracked*, flat and vindictively. The Texan was lit-

erally knocked out of his saddle by the force of the
.30-30 slug from Caleb Masters's carbine. The remaining two Whiting riders whirled their horses
with blinding speed and dug in the spurs. They
had overlooked the possibility of the Circle L riders
having rifles. The dead Texan's horse ran, head up
and stirrups flapping, behind the retreating cowboys.

Buff felt the breath of the pistol shot as the slug narrowly missed him. He winced involuntarily. Whiting's eyes focused slowly, and the two men stood
facing one another for a long, silent moment. Slim
and the Masters boys were watching the pantomime
from the safety of their horse-carcass fortification.

"One more chance, Whiting." Buff's voice had lost
a little of its fire. "Are you goin' to pay fer the feed or
fill your hand?"

Whiting's neck was turning a vivid purple and
blood still ran from the murderous blow along the
side of his face. He was in agony, and he ran a badly
shaking hand gingerly over his battered face. "You
go to hell." The words were hoarse and forced.

Buff's bony knuckles flashed into a hard fist and
the piston-like swing of his arm looked slow and
lazy to the watchers. Its speed was deceptive, and,
when it connected with Whiting's face, the echo
sounded like the report of a small-caliber pistol.

Again Whiting went down. This time he was still,
and the rasping sound of his breath was harsh and
ragged through the welling gush of blood that filled
his mouth from a badly smashed nose.

Slim jumped up with a torrent of wild profanity
and dashed headlong toward his brother. Buff was
wounded, but at least he was capable of standing in
one place and giving battle. Whiting had been out

on his feet when Buff struck him. At best he was no match for Buff, dulled and badly hurt from the quirting; he was in no condition to fight at all. Buff heard his brother coming and faced about. His eyes mirrored surprise and a little misgiving. Never before in his life had the elder Liskey seen Slim's face show such unrestrained savagery. Instinctively Buff let his right hand drop to the holstered .45.

For once the passion of the elder Liskey brother was overwhelmed, and his savagery quailed before the fury of his younger brother. He opened his mouth to say something but Slim was on him. Buff ducked and feinted under the barrage of wild and lightning-like blows from his younger brother. Slim's pent-up anger had finally broken the head gates of control and was flooding his veins with unadulterated fury. Buff threw two looping lefts, missed with the first one, but raised a red welt on Slim's cheek with the other. Slim backed off, parried two murderous jabs, and fired an overhand punch that rocked Buff back on his heels. Seeing his opportunity, Slim stepped in close and cut loose with a right and left to the stomach that brought Buff into a snarling, gasping crouch in spite of himself. Then Slim rose on his toes and put all his weight into a blasting uppercut that straightened Buff up, rigid, for a long moment. His unconscious body began to sag, just when the violent roar of a six-gun shattered the deathly still atmosphere.

When the gun went off, Slim was watching his brother; he saw the lean, powerful body jerk spasmodically, twist sideways a little, and plummet to the ground, a welter of dark blood bubbling out of a jagged hole in his chest.

Incredulous, Slim turned around and saw

Whiting—his face a gory wreck, out of which two feverish eyes glowed amid the caked blood and swollen flesh—raising his Peacemaker for the second shot. Slim grabbed desperately for his own gun, swung it in a short arc—raising the hammer as the gun was brought to bear—and squeezed the trigger. Not waiting to see the effect of his first shot, Slim fired again and again. The thunderous roar of the short-barreled man-killer blasted the funereal quiet that had settled over Grass Valley since the Circle L cowboys and Whiting's Texans were held spellbound.

Whiting was dead. Out of three shots Slim had pumped at him, two had been lodged lethally in his body. Buff Liskey was dead. Whiting's only shot had entered Buff's back below the shoulder blade, angled around, and blown his heart out in front. Sheriff Carter arose from examining both bodies, and faced Slim.

"If I'd been just ten minutes sooner, Slim, this wouldn't have happened."

Slim nodded dully, and the sheriff shrugged. "Well, that there Whiting cowboy that was locked up with you last night, he run out on his pals there an' come a-roarin' into town fer me, but I reckon he didn't start soon enough." The sheriffs calloused and philosophical glance ran over the two dead men again. "Danged if that Whiting feller wasn't pretty well used up anyway, by the looks of his face." He raised his eyebrows questioningly. "You do it?"

Slim shook his head, and the sheriff nodded and clucked gently. "I should've known Buff done it." Again he shrugged. "Well, good thing I brought a posse. Them two are too heavy fer me to tie onto horses alone."

There was a long silence, then Sheriff Carter turned to Slim and the hardness in his eyes was gone. "Go on home, Slim. If I need you, I'll send you word."

Slim and the Masters boys rode in silence into the yard of the Circle L. Dusk was spreading a velvet blanket of cool shadows like a gentle benediction over the harsh outlines and square corners of the buildings and corrals. In silence Caleb stoked the fire in the temperamental old kitchen range while Sam put up the stock and did the chores. Slim leaned against the old log barn his father had built many years before and its bleached, solid old front was warm and comforting. Buff gone. It had to happen, though, someday. Buff had lived longer than most quick-tempered men at that; he was in his middle forties when Whiting's slug had cut him down. It wasn't exactly mourning that filled Slim's soul. It was the fact that he was the last and only member of his family left on earth.

Slim rolled a cigarette unconsciously and lit it. There was a rustle in the gloom off to his left and he wildly dropped the match, spat out the cigarette, jumped sideways into the barn, and his battered old .45 leaped magically into his hand.

Slim's palms were wet, his eyes wide in their effort to pierce the deepening shadow. Again the noise came jerkily, like the sound of a barefoot horse walking in thick dust. Slim relaxed a trifle. The sound probably came from one of the corrals at the side of the barn. There were horses over there. Tiptoeing silently to the door of the barn, Slim peered around the edge of the cavernous opening and came face to face with a girl. He started violently and the gun hammer *clicked* ominously. Then, seeing the girl staring at him, wide-eyed, he turned a deep crimson and was thankful for the dusk that hid it.

"Is that the way you folks at the Circle L greet people?" The voice was hostile and had the throaty sweetness of a mountain stream tumbling over shiny pebbles.

Slim holstered the gun surreptitiously and his hands felt as large as tree stumps. "Uh, ma'am . . . I thought you might be someone else. You see, there was a fight today."

The girl interrupted as she finished tying her horse and walked toward him. "I know. I'm Christel Carter. Dad told me about it. I met him going into town while I was out riding and he suggested that I come up here and cook for you boys tonight."

Slim nodded eagerly, anything to get away from discussing his hasty action with the gun. "Well, that's mighty nice of your dad. Matter-of-fact, I guess I heard the boys tryin' to hustle some food a minute ago. I'm sure of it, 'cause I just heard Caleb cussin' like a . . . well, that is, I think Caleb's tryin' to make the stove work now, judgin' from the sounds comin' from the kitchen."

The girl tossed her head and a wealth of auburn hair tumbled out from under her Stetson. "Well, show me the kitchen then, and I'll see if I can help."

Slim didn't hear the words at all. This was Sheriff Carter's daughter. He shook his head ever so slightly. How did that garrulous old wood tick ever have anything like this around, let alone raise it without him knowing it. Why, she was beautiful. Her eyes were dark brown and large and the pert little nose with the barely perceptible etching of freckles across its bridge and the wide, generous mouth. Again he shook his head ever so slightly. She wasn't tall, maybe not more than five feet, two inches, but Nature hadn't skimped; her figure was full and round and strong.

Slim was lost in his trance when the girl turned an impatient eye his way. "Well, do we go to the kitchen or don't we?" Slim yanked himself back to reality with an effort and flushed anew as he realized that he had been staring.

"Yes, sure . . . ah . . . follow me." He started off across the yard still in a trance. The girl tossed him a peculiar look, shrugged, and followed. Slim turned to look again, his boot struck an old wagon wheel that had been lying in that exact spot since he had been a small boy. In fact, he had played with the thing for as far back as he could remember. There was a grinding *clatter*, a sharply exhaled breath, and a loud *thump* as Slim went his length on the ground.

Christel Carter eyed him critically for a second, bent over, and smiled. "Are you hurt?"

Slim looked up in confusion and embarrassment—and grabbed at the implication. "Well, I might be at that. Would you help me up?" Restraining a wise smile that was hidden by the shadows, Christel extended her slender, cool hand and Slim's calloused, sinewy fingers found it, held on, and, as he came to his feet, he continued to hold on. He grinned nervously. "Let's go. I reckon I'm all right, but a fall like that might affect a man's eyesight . . . so, if you don't mind, I'll keep hold of your hand."

Christel smiled impishly and looked up at him in the gloom. "I don't mind at all. Besides, as dark as it's getting, I might get lost without someone to guide me." There was a moment of silence, then Caleb Masters started suddenly and raised astounded eyebrows as he heard a man and a woman laugh heartily in the darkness outside the kitchen window.

The Dark Avenger

I

Brade Ballard wasn't a man who smiled often or easily. There was nothing especially unpleasant about him, unless it was his peculiar aura of wolfishness that could be felt rather than seen. He stood under six feet in his boots with the heavily silvered *Californio* spurs; the full length of his body was hard and full, with the appearance of muscle packed and punched down under the swarthiness of his skin. He wore two guns, and a flat-topped hat with a stiff brim, and his face, with the long, sensitive nose, was an etching of a man to whom life was real. He had black eyes and a thin mouth. Any of the men in the Anglica Saloon in Chiqui saw that in a glance, and they left him alone. With a stranger in Chiqui, that was the best way.

Jim Travis gauged the stranger as was the custom. A new man in town—any frontier town—was measured as a matter of course. It was necessary. Sometimes a man's life depended on his guessing right; sometimes someone else's life, for the trails were ripe with all manner of men, not the least of whom were paid killers. Far worse were men who rode on a trail of hate all their own. Jim guessed the dark man to be one of these—a lone wolf hunting an enemy. There was that look about Brade Ballard.

Sometimes folks called Travis "Silent Jim". He wasn't talkative—normally. With a low, broad forehead and chestnut hair that clung in large curls under the summer sweat of his floppy hat, Jim drank a tepid ale in the Anglica and moodily studied the people. It was late afternoon. The sun was reluctantly surrendering to cool shadows, and the great range was almost sighing with a fragrant whisper that brought the smell of pines and sage and juniper to the heat-blistered town.

Jim looked at Chiqui and thought of the mighty War Bonnet beyond, where Samuel Barbera ruled his empire of cattle and horses and hard-eyed riders like a king, and bitterness lay back in the depths of his blue eyes. Barbera was a power in the Chiqui range. He owned . . . well—Jim drank the last of his ale.—it didn't matter, he owned everything. Two-thirds of Chiqui. The bank, almost, and all the land, clean to the Mexican line. He was more of a legend than a man, and for that reason Travis felt no qualms over what happened to the man or his War Bonnet outfit.

But there was this other thing, this damned smuggling over the line. Jim had tried to see Barbera without luck. He had written him, without answer, and now he was going to trespass, regardless of the blunt warnings of the local men. Travis's job was to stop the smuggling. For that reason alone, he had been sent to Chiqui. He saw a tall, whisker-stubbled cowboy he had met the day before, when he'd been riding the land, getting the lay of it. The man rode for Ned Hawk's Muleshoe outfit, north of Chiqui about seventeen miles. His name was Merton, Jim remembered that, Alvin Merton. He sidled over and nodded.

Merton nodded back and made a wry face. "Gawd awful hot, ain't it?"

"Damn if it isn't. Day off?"

"Naw. I brought in the wagon. Supplies from Liddell's store." Merton studied him through squinted eyes. "You trespass yet?" Travis shook his head slowly and Merton nodded. "Take the advice I give you yesterday at the salt licks. Don't."

"Like I said . . . it's open range, isn't it?"

"Don't cut no ice, pardner . . . not with War Bonnet. They make their own law. No fences an' no trespassin'."

"Anyone ever try to fence?"

Merton let the ale run down his scorched gullet before he answered. "Yas. Once. Homesteaders. They didn't last a month. Burned out, shot out, and run out." He put the mug down and half turned toward Jim. "It's like this. Ol' Sam'l Barbera says he owns the gawd-damned land an' ain't nobody else got a right on it." With a shrug. "That's right, but most cowmen don't look at it quite like he does." Another shrug. "But the facts're the same. Barbera's the biggest, wealthiest, hardest cowman in these parts. His word's law, pardner, an' he backs her up."

"How?"

"With a beatin' first, then, if that don't work, a bullet." Merton's eyes flicked to the dark man at the upper end of the bar. He hesitated, stared, then let his eyes drop to the bar top. "Who in hell's that up there? That real dark gent with the skinny nose?"

Jim knew who he meant but didn't look. "Hell, I don't know." He turned away. "S'long, Merton. Time for my supper."

"S'long."

Travis ate at the Chinese café, drifted through the cool night to the Parker House. He went to his room on the ground floor and lay awake for a long time, thinking, half deaf to the rising sounds of revelry. It wasn't like smuggling guns; that was difficult and dangerous, and all but discouraged now. This was better all around—smuggling cheap gold out of Mexico into the States—where it sold for much more than in Mexico and was good business. Profitable business. Unlike guns, there was no maker's name or trademark to trace. All gold looked the same, and sneaking it over the line was becoming increasingly popular because the bankrupt Mexican government couldn't and wouldn't pay a big price for the stuff, while the American government would.

Travis turned things over in his mind. It didn't sound like the work of cowboys, or even the small ranchers who lived along the border. Somehow he suspected that a merchant's mind was behind it, someone who knew values and commercial outlets. It just didn't make sense to Jim Travis, that none—or very little—of the gold was ever peddled in Chiqui or the other border towns. That, more than anything else, made him suspect a sound business organization—a merchant's guidance, not a cowman's. He turned up on one side and shrugged irritably. It was necessary to trespass on War Bonnet land to study the border where the stuff was probably brought over. He'd hoped to be able to make Barbera see it that way, but the man wasn't interested. Jim would have to trespass, which, he'd learned, was Barbera's first hate. War Bonnet's reasoning was sound—no trespassing, no rustling.

Dawn was the sweetest time of the day. It held warmth and fragrant coolness, plus soft light and silence. Jim rode down the immense swell of dead land and smelled the Digger pines and shaggy old junipers. Rabbits were out feeding and an occasional sage hen waddled off at his advance, but the land was as quiet, as motionless and peaceful as heaven must be.

The sun turned from a blessing of delicate pink to a sphere of malevolent yellow that burned the sky into a faded, shimmering, brassy blue before Travis came to the little trails that wound across the border. Twice he found the signs marking the line, shot-riddled and bleaching on the ground; for the two miles between them, traffic had been heavy. He was studying the small hoof marks on his knees, noticing how they were unshod and apparently made by burros, when the full blast of the summer sun rolled over the land, bleaching the moisture and dew from plant and animal alike. He straightened up thoughtfully. Here quite likely—not more than eight miles from Chiqui—was where the greatest number of smugglers came across. Evidently they drove burros laden with their contraband.

Travis mounted, flicked the sweat off his nose, and reined back for town. He had to meet more of the merchants in Chiqui. The thought persisted that a more commercially-minded man than a cowboy or a rancher was behind this thing.

He hadn't traveled far—perhaps two miles—when he saw four riders coming toward him slowly, heads up and eyes staring. There was a sensation of wariness rising within Travis even before he saw the skeletal outline of a War Bonnet on their horses' left shoulders.

The men stopped, barring his path, a silent, grim-faced lot. One rider, younger than the others, kneed out a few feet and ignored Jim's nod. There was open hostility in the sun-darkened face with its slate-gray eyes and full, heavy mouth. Jim measured this man;

he knew instinctively that this was the leader. About Travis's own size, he was leaner, and possibly three years younger. The great silver buckle of his shell belt, and the silver conchos on his saddle spelled money.

Jim didn't nod a second time. "Howdy."

The younger man ignored it, studying him. "Stranger, you're trespassin'."

"Open range country?"

"Not on War Bonnet land."

Jim saw the suppressed wrath and met it calmly, glance for glance. "You got special laws hereabouts?"

"For eighty miles, stranger, everyone knows War Bonnet's no trespassin' laws."

"An' if a man doesn't know about 'em?" Travis knew, the instant he said it, he had been baited. The man's eyes gleamed unmercifully. He nodded for the first time. "Then we teach him!"

Jim watched his small, gloved hand flicker to a wispy man on a breedy sorrel gelding. It was a signal. The wizened cowboy nudged out, flashed a gun, and fired. Travis saw the motion toward the gun and flashed for his own, but his horse was falling even as he palmed it, shot dead by the wiry cowboy. He kicked free of the stirrups and leaped aside; the horse quivered once, threshed, and lay still, a torrent of sticky claret cascading out his nose. Travis's fury burned white-hot and wild within him. He tilted the gun muzzle and looked up into four cocked pistols. It was useless.

The leader of the War Bonnet riders was somberly looking down at him. "You got an eight-mile hike packing your saddle, mister. That's plenty of time to think it over. No trespassin' on War Bonnet!" He holstered his gun, reined around, and rode off, northwest. The riders followed.

Jim Travis had never sniped a man, but the impulse was like fire in him as he watched the broad backs riding off. A long, ragged breath slid over his cracked, compressed lips, then he holstered his gun, unsaddled the dead horse, cached the saddle, and struck out for town. It was a blistering, maddening walk, with the full force of the murderous sun beating down, buffeting him with killing rays and sucking the sweat off his body before it touched his shirt. Spirals of rage whirled up with each irregular, panting beat of his heart until the landscape was tinted a faint red around the rims of his narrowed, watering eyes. He didn't see the horseman following him, nor would he have understood when Brade Ballard scooped up his saddle, balanced it on one hip, and struck off behind him at a discreet distance, brooding-eyed and venomous.

Chiqui, for all its squalor and refuse and myriad stem-winding bluebottle flies, was a wonderful vision to Travis's dehydrated body. He swung up stiffly onto the plank walk, where it ended and the raw range began, and stomped solidly toward the Anglica Saloon. He knew men looked at him as he passed, and he also knew that he was a sorry sight, with the coating of gray dust and caked salt stiffening his faded shirt, and the small, bloody cracks along his stiff lips. What he didn't realize was that the murder that had turned his heart black showed in his sunken steely eyes. The men were used to dried sweat and dust and broken lips every day, but they weren't accustomed to the fury they saw.

"Ale."

The bartender set it up, watched Jim down it, refilled, and watched that one disappear more slowly. The third, however, just sat there, with one mahogany claw gripping it. He turned back to his other customers.

II

Gordo Tomas's moon face, glistening with a greasy sort of perspiration, watched as the husky, very dark man dumped a saddle in the unkempt alleyway of his livery barn. He blinked at the wooden face of the man, waiting. Coal-black eyes ate into him; he could feel them going to his heart and beyond—to his soul. He smiled. Gordo, for all his great pendulous belly, thick arms and shoulders, and spindly legs of a born horseman avoided trouble the way most men avoided the noonday sun.

"Belongs to a *hombre* named Travis. He's up at the Anglica. Send him word, *paisano*. Don't say how it got here. Understand?"

Gordo's flat-brimmed sombrero over the rank, coarse nest of black hair, nodded quickly. "*Sí, amigo. It is here, for Travis, but . . . ¿quién sabe? . . . who knows how or why?*"

The dark man nodded and rode on out of the barn. Gordo watched him ride south, past the constable's office, and swing west at the end of town. He shrugged. His part in the thing was small and he would fulfill it, but beyond that—no more. He beckoned to a half-breed urchin who was laboriously braiding a small reata in the fly-laden atmosphere of the shady manure pile, near the rear maw of the barn. "*Muchacho, en aquí. ¡Venga!*"

* * *

Jim Travis hauled up the buckets for a bath and winced as he drew off his boots. There was a magnificent blister on his right heel, the size of a quarter. He bathed glumly, dried himself, and dressed in stiff new Levi's and butternut shirt, dumped the black bath water, and smoked in the shade of the over-hang outside of the Parker House. The bath made a difference. The resentment remained, as resolved, as eternal and solid as ever, but the savagery was gone. It went with the daylight scorch and mellowed with the coming of another late, shadowy afternoon.

He ate a big supper at 3:30, and went back to the coolness of the hotel's overhang. He was still there when three riders jogged arrogantly down the dusty, manure-laden thoroughfare. They rode from the north end of town. Jim held the cigarette, forgotten as he watched them approach. He recognized them easily enough. One was the sulky-looking leader of the men who had shot his horse, and the others were two of the cowboys who had backed him up. He watched them ride by, like proud rulers, and swing down outside the Anglica.

Travis's first impulse was to call the War Bonnet cowboys, one at a time. Then a wily thought oc-curred to him. Now would be a wonderful opportu-nity to prowl the War Bonnet itself. The riders were in town—most of them, anyway—and the mellow light of a nearly full moon would help him. He stamped out the cigarette, got up, and went across to Tomas's livery barn, rented a horse, and found his saddle where he'd hung it after the urchin had told him where it was, saddled up, swung aboard, and rode out into the still warm night.

The livery horse was a good animal. Gordo To-mas was a born horseman in more ways than one;

he fed and cared for his animals. Silent, Jim Travis cut southwestward and rode for close to an hour before he saw orange squares ahead in the gloom. He rode closer, reined up, and sat still, studying the orderly buildings of the War Bonnet headquarters. There were three great log barns. A long bunkhouse with a rambling cook shack behind it. A regular galaxy of pole corrals, chutes, and log squeezes, and—a little apart—was the large, low house of the legendary emperor of the huge Chiqui country. It was unmistakable. There were broad verandahs and large windows, and flowers. Here was the nest of the mightiest eagle of them all.

Jim smiled thinly to himself. If he bearded the man in his own den—what then? Another dead horse? No, Merton had said first a beating, which he hadn't gotten, then a bullet. He spat to one side sourly. It wouldn't be so easy the second time. A warned man was an armed man; Jim Travis was both. He lifted the reins to ride down to the big, low house, when a voice stopped him rigidly in the saddle.

"Hold it *hombre*. Not a move."

Jim sat like a statue, cursing to himself. The damned place must be guarded like a fort? Why? He heard the spurs jingling softly as a man came up behind him, jerked his gun out, tossed it down, and stepped back.

"Get down!"

Jim obeyed.

"Turn around."

He turned, eyes widening in surprise. It wasn't a man at all; it was a tall, lithe girl with golden hair gathered into a ribboned, soft ponytail behind her head, under a dove-gray Stetson with gracefully up-curving outer edges.

"What're you doing on War Bonnet land?"

Jim didn't answer right away. She was nearly as tall as he was, in spite of the silver-buttoned moccasins on her small, broad feet. She was firm-breasted and narrow-waisted, with a swell to her hips that showed under the tight Levi's. His eyes went, then, to her face, and the jet black eyes in the creamy skin were startling. Even more so was the handsome mouth, large, full-lipped and graceful with a sensitive, slightly humorous upper lip. He smiled gently. "Lookin' for something, ma'am."

"Find it?"

He nodded slowly. "Yes. I think so." He flagged an arm toward the buildings behind him. "The headquarters of the War Bonnet."

"War Bonnet doesn't need riders, stranger, and doesn't take to trespassers."

"So I've heard," he said dryly.

"Then what're you doing here, sneaking around at night?"

"Not sneaking, ma'am. Just wondering what'd happen if I went down and demanded to see Barbera."

Her ebony eyes had a saturnine look. "You're going to find out, mister. Turn around." She waved her carbine at him, motioning toward the buildings. He didn't move. She frowned a little. "Did you hear me?"

"Yes'm."

"Then turn."

"No'm."

The look in her handsome face was harsh and unpleasant. He heard the dog snap back on the carbine. "I'm not fooling, cowboy."

"Me, either, ma'am."

"You . . . damned fool." The finger was cuddled around the trigger like a small, sinewy snake.

Jim saw it and wondered at the wisdom of his stand. "War Bonnet's hard up for men. Usin' women sentinels."

She didn't answer. Indecision was in her eyes, but not in the cold set of her jaw.

He shrugged. Impasse. "I'll make a trade with you, ma'am. If you'll answer three questions for me, I'll go down there with you. Otherwise, you can pull the trigger and be damned."

There was a brittle silence, then she licked her lips. That was all he needed.

"First . . . who are you?"

"Linda Barbera."

"Samuel's daughter?"

"Yes."

"Thanks. Two . . . who's a young buck with a big silver buckle on his shell belt? Rides War Bonnet horses?"

"Jack Talbert. My cousin. He's foreman here since my brother left."

Jim nodded. "Thanks again. Now one more . . . why won't War Bonnet allow trespassing?"

"That should be easy. No strangers, no rustling. No trespassing allowed, no trouble from the outside."

Jim frowned slightly. "Why outside, ma'am? War Bonnet got trouble inside?"

"That's four, stranger."

Jim almost smiled. He nodded at her thoughtfully. "All right, I'll stick to the bargain." He started to turn, hesitated, and looked back at her. "War Bonnet killed my horse today, Linda. Do they ever pay damages?"

She walked close and prodded him over the kidneys with the gun. "You were lucky, mister. Usually they do worse to trespassers."

Jim turned without another word, caught the reins of the livery horse, and walked stolidly toward the ranch yard. There was a reason, then, why Jack Talbert hadn't had him beaten. A badly used-up man could never last the eight miles to Chiqui. He grunted to himself. It was clever at that. By the time he'd gotten back to town, he was as battered and bruised—and blistered—as though he'd been trounced, anyway.

"Toward the house. Leave the horse here."

He looped the reins once around the hitch rail and walked on across the yard, up onto the roofed-over verandah, where the smell of honeysuckle and sage was overpowering, and stopped.

"Rap."

Jim knuckled the door and watched as it opened. A small, aging woman stood blinking out at him for a second, then she turned away without a greeting and jerked her head.

"Samuel."

But Barbera didn't get there before the girl prodded him inside. Then he was face to face with the man who held the lives and fortunes of the Chiqui range in his fist. And it was quite a fist, at that.

Barbera was short, squatty, massive. His face was aloof and cold, and wore the serene half-contemptuous, half-ruthless look of a man born to power. Their eyes held. Both blue and icy, then Barbera's appraisal was over. He turned to the lithesome girl without a word, waiting. She leaned the carbine against the wall, tossed her hat on a table, and nodded toward Travis. "Found him sitting on the range looking over the buildings. Alone."

Barbera's smoky eyes came back, hostile. "Trespassing, stranger?"

Jim had made his mind up that he wasn't going through that routine again. He fished in his pocket and held out his palm. Barbera's glance dropped for a second, but the cold look didn't alter. His voice was the same, hard and impersonal.

"So?"

"Smuggling. I'm here to. . . ."

"Not on War Bonnet, you're not, mister." The aloof eyes held on Travis's face. "No trespassing means that and no more. *No trespassing.* That goes for lawmen, cowmen, soldiers . . . even the President himself. If you have smugglers to contend with, mister, you'll do it without trespassing on the War Bonnet. Do you understand?"

Travis's wrath was boiling up. "Even if the smugglers are using the enforcement of your no trespassing law to work without fear of interruption?"

Barbera nodded once curtly. "Even then, mister. If smugglers are trespassing, *I'll* teach them a lesson, not you. Anyway, I don't believe you."

Jim saw the iron resolve staring out of the cold eyes at him. It left him with a definite sensation of nullity. He couldn't reason with the man, that was obvious. He was face to face with the unwritten law of the Chiqui country, and it wasn't subject to reason, logic—or anything else. He looked past the powerful man to the small, drab woman behind him, watching impassively. He noticed her black eyes, like two brilliant pools of oil and the creamy darkness of her skin, and knew where the handsome daughter got her coloring.

His thoughts were jerked back to reality when Samuel Barbera spoke again. "Mister, you've come to the house and have immunity because of it . . . even though you didn't come voluntarily. You will ride away unharmed. But I promise you, lawman or no lawman, I'll give orders in the morning that, if you're caught on the War Bonnet again, you're to be treated as any other trespasser. Is that clear?"

Jim didn't answer right away. He let his contempt show in his face for a moment, then he turned abruptly and started for the door. "You're a little behind the times, *hombre*. Now you're going to find it out."

He slammed the door and stalked angrily across the yard to his horse, untied it, and was toeing the stirrup when he saw the wispy shadow beside the hitch rail and recognized the man who had shot his horse.

Jim swung up and glared down at the shadow. "Pardner, I'm waiting for you to show up in Chiqui." He whirled without getting an answer, and rode back the way he had come.

III

There was a bench outside of the blacksmith's shop, next to the abstract office and directly across from the raucous Anglica Saloon. It was in darkness. Jim Travis sat on it and smoked. Orders to run the gold smugglers to earth were expected; as a Ranger he was used to things like this. But the hostility of the War Bonnet complicated things. He could send for help, of course, but that wasn't the way he worked. He exhaled a gust of smoke and grunted under his breath. This was the first time he'd ever had both the forces of right and wrong aligned against him.

Barbara was within his rights, up to a point. But his refusal to co-operate with the law made it a peculiar situation. Jim knew the War Bonnet wasn't in on the smuggling. What would a man who had everything—and had gotten it legally—want with more wealth that he didn't need? Why would he sneak to get it? No, Barbera was just a ruthless cowman—a product of an earlier era—and he made things very awkward.

Travis got up and started toward the constable's office, then stopped. Three men stamped out of the Anglica and stood on the duckboards, carelessly making strollers go around them. He recognized them as the War Bonnet men he'd seen earlier, and his mouth drew down. The riders seemed to be discussing something, then the younger man with the flashing silver belt buckle threw back his head and laughed. It had a nasty, grating sound that jangled on Jim's backbone. Angry and resentful before, Jack Talbert's laugh brought up his gorge of fury. Without thinking, he swung off the duckboards, stalked through the filth of the street, and approached the War Bonnet men. If they saw him coming, it meant nothing. Not until he was close, then his voice made them squint into the shadows of the night.

"Talbert!"

The foreman turned his head but not his body; the arrogant eyes were baleful. That was Jack Talbert's first mistake. Jim's hand caught his shirt and yanked savagely. Talbert went off balance, staggered out into the dusty roadway, and felt a blasting numbness high on the side of his head, then a thick, encompassing vortex of red and black light carried him downward. When his face smashed into the filth, he didn't feel the pain. There was a thin streamer of blood, whipped upward from the edge of his mouth onto one pale cheek.

Jim looked at the War Bonnet cowboys, dumbfounded and rigid. "Second blood, boys. War Bonnet got first this mornin'." He was watching them closely and didn't see Brade Ballard leaning against the saloon, behind them, one hand resting easily on his gun, the other hand holding a dead cigarette. Jim nodded toward Talbert. "Haul him away, boys." He was turning back toward the constable's office when he spoke again. "Let's see who gets third blood."

Jim was walking back across the roadway, wide shoulders swinging in contempt, when one of the Barbera riders dipped for his gun. His little eyes were murderous. "I'll kill the son— . . . !"

"Try it, cowboy!"

The man took his hand away from the gun, half drawn, and twisted his head. Brade Ballard's hands both held guns, cocked and pointing belly low. The dead cigarette was gone; the swarthy face nodded under the wild glitter in the black eyes. "Go ahead. Try it, you filthy scum."

Jack Talbert groaned. It was the only close sound over the racket of the saloon's patrons.

Again the dark head nodded. "I'll remember your faces, boys. You got the rest of the night to leave the Chiqui country. By dawn I'll be out huntin' you. Shoot on sight, boys, because I will." The guns disappeared. "Get your garbage, War Bonnet, and git!"

The cowboys scooped up a wobbly Jack Talbert, and left town.

Constable Elmore nodded in silence as Jim Travis talked, then he spoke. "Yeah, I've heard there's smugglin' along the line. Heard it ever since I was a shaver." He shrugged. "Except fer the town, though, I got no authority."

"How about War Bonnet?"

Elmore's face looked pained. "Barbera's ruled this country for a long time, Ranger. A long time. I've been sick of his damned high-handedness for quite a while. Still, he's never bucked the law before." He smiled thinly. "Of course the law's never stepped on his toes, either."

Jim nodded bleakly. "All right, Constable. I told you the facts for just one reason. If anything happens to me . . . or the War Bonnet riders that jump me . . . you'll know the lay of the land."

The constable watched the husky Ranger get up

and noticed his hard look. "All right, son, I understand. Insofar as I can, I'll he'p you, but don't ask the impossible."

"I won't, Constable."

Gordo Tomas was asleep in a chair padded with stinking horse blankets when Jim shook him. He blinked furiously, then slid his customary smile up onto his face with no meaning. *"Sí, señor. ¿Sí?"*

"The same horse I had before."

Gordo grunted erect. His feet had swollen in the boots and he swore uncomfortably as he hobbled out into the feebly lit alleyway of the barn.

Jim rode northwest again, across the War Bonnet. He had a long detour that carried him past the War Bonnet buildings, saw only the sallow light from the bunkhouse's lantern with its eternally untrimmed wick, then he swung due east, by-passed Chiqui, and swung down along the border until he was close to the downed markers. Here he left the horse, his spurs buckled around the saddle horn, and went on afoot. It was grueling work and he grunted over the small irritation of the broken blister on his heel, but suddenly it paid off.

In the shadow world ahead he saw a string of doleful little burros plodding patiently along, single file, with worn *alforjas* strapped to them.

Jim's mouth was like cotton. He hunkered in the soft, moist light and counted. Seven burros, but no drivers. He waited until the small *clop-clop* was faint in the distance, then he jogged back, caught his horse, and swung up.

Following the burros wasn't easy. The faint silhouette of a mounted man, moving against the stillness of the range, was easily seen by watching eyes. He

finally left the horse in a chokecherry thicket and
trudged along afoot until he saw the animals somberly walk into the deserted and tumble-down old
corral beside a long dead ranch of bleached, bedrag-
gled wood, and calmly start munching at a heaping
grain and hay manger. Two men came forward without sound, from the old barn, and began the unsaddling and unpacking of the small animals. Jim had
seen enough; he dared not push his luck. He re-
traced his steps, swung back onto his rented animal,
and rode thoughtfully back toward Chiqui. That
much was solved.

Someone, over the line, in Mexico, loaded the animals and turned them loose. Grained and fed the
choicest feed, the little burros immediately returned
across the border to their home corrals. It was good.
All the Rangers in Texas could wait at the border
and arrest the smugglers as they trooped home-
ward, but whoever heard of prosecuting seven sad-
eyed little burros?

By the time Travis turned the animal back over to
Gordo Tomas, he was perilously close to a smile.
The night had been productive; he forgot the bitter-
ness of earlier and went to his room.

Samuel Barbera listened to Jack Talbert's version of
why two of the War Bonnet riders drew their money
and rode. There was an odd look in his pale blue
eyes and he kept letting them slide off Talbert's
bruised face to the impassive, jet black eyes of his
wife, who sat perfectly still at the breakfast table,
listening. Finally he waved a hand abruptly at his
foreman.

"All right, Jack. We'll take the boys into Chiqui
later on and throw some weight around. Can't have

things like this happening. Hard on War Bonnet's prestige." His face went up again. "Did you try an' talk 'em out of quittin'?"

"Yeah." Talbert's words were thick past the swelling of his mouth and jaw. "But they got no heart fer it."

"All right. That's all. I'll be out later."

Jack left and Samuel Barbera avoided his wife's stare and ate slowly. He knew Linda's eyes, so like her mother's, were stabbing at him, too. He didn't think she'd speak, though, and, when she did, he was nettled more than surprised. "It must've been that same man. The Ranger."

He grunted. "I'll take care of that."

His wife spoke then, in her strained soft voice. A quarter of a century of hard domination had made her like that. "But . . . this other man, Samuel."

His cold eyes glared. He seemed on the verge of saying something, then just shook his head harshly, threw down his napkin, and left the table. Linda reached over and squeezed her mother's hand. She knew what lay behind those other black eyes. Her brother, missing for close to seven years, disowned by his father for crossing him. Linda left, too. She saddled her horse and rode aimlessly. The blasting, smashing sun was no detriment; she'd never known anything else.

Jim Travis arose late, ate, then strolled casually over to the hot shade of the bench by the blacksmith's shop and turned his discovery over in his mind. He saw the long-nosed, black-eyed two-gun man ride down through the early heat and swing in at the blacksmith shop, and wondered about him idly. There was something about the man—he shrugged,

too much else on his mind right now. Then he saw
Frank Liddell, the wealthy young trader who owned
the largest mercantile store in Chiqui—Liddel's
Emporium—leading a handsome bay gelding toward the forge, and a thought struck him.

Liddell was youngish, thin-lipped, like a bear
trap, with genial, deep-set eyes, and a quick, insis-
tent way about him. He was smart enough, all right.

Jim's eyes narrowed as he slouched on the bench.
He watched Liddell through the lashes and specu-
lated. Tonight he'd go deeper into the thing. He'd
hide in the barn in the early afternoon and wait. It
made him wince; he'd have to turn his horse loose
to avoid detection and that meant another eight
mile hike across the range—this time with a blister
already on his right foot. He was grinning to himself when he looked up and felt his eyes drop into a
pair of stony, black eyes atop a handsome gray
horse.

Linda Barbera felt the raw heat on her shoulders
as she looked down at the Ranger; there was a self-
satisfied smirk on his face that annoyed her. Then,
when he looked up and saw her staring at him, it left.
There was just the startled, surprised look in his blue
eyes, but she had seen the other look.

"Feeling smug today, Mister Ranger?"

Jim looked at her with unveiled admiration. Tall
in the saddle, lithe and wholesome. He felt something more than admiration. She was beautiful here,
in her native habitat. He would have put her nowhere else; she wouldn't fit. Just here, in open range
cow country.

He shrugged. "No reason not to, ma'am . . . uh . . .
Linda."

She flicked her reins just as Frank Liddell walked

up with his led horse and smiled up at her. "Hi, sweetheart. Have lunch with me?"

There was spite in her voice, and it was louder than it had to be. "Glad to, Frank, soon's I have my horse's shoes re-set."

Jim didn't see the triumphant glare she fired at him. He was looking at Frank Liddell. "Lunch," Liddell had said. In the country lunch was called dinner, and the city man's dinner was called supper. Liddell was a city man, originally.

Jim stowed that away with other little things he'd seen or heard. There were several items in his mind, but they still didn't make sense. Not yet, but he felt they would soon. He could have all the suspicions he wanted, but suspicions had never caught a man yet, to his knowledge. He'd have to get something more solid. He lifted his eyes, watched the girl dismount, disdaining Liddell's offer of a hand, and felt the funny little sensation again. She was just about perfect—even over a carbine barrel in the moonlight.

That reminded him. Tonight it would be a full moon; he had to get to the old deserted ranch early. He fished listlessly for the tobacco sack and made another quirly, lit it, and looked up at the shadow standing at the end of the bench, watching him. It was the constable.

"Howdy, Elmore. Have a seat."

The lawman sat and squinted at Travis. "I saw that look Linda gave you. You aren't very popular in that quarter, I reckon."

"No," Jim drawled with a pensive look. "Not very. In fact, I punched a little stuffin' out of her cousin, Jack Talbert, last night, after goin' to the War Bonnet and arguin' with her pa. I don't reckon she's got any call to love me." His breath went out of him when he unconsciously said the last two words and the strange sensation came back with a roar that made his ears ring. He puffed quickly on the cigarette to hide the sudden revelation.

Elmore began to whittle a stick. "Ranger, I smell trouble for you in Chiqui."

"I'm not surprised."

"But . . . you got a friend, too."

"Who?"

"It don't matter . . . can't say exactly. But after the news got around you punched Talbert silly, well, sir, you suddenly had a friend. *Hombre* I've knowed all of his life. Makes a damned fine friend, too, believe me."

Jim ground out the cigarette. "Well," he said, arising, "if this is your day for riddles, Constable, you'll have to answer 'em for yourself. Personally I never cared for 'em." He turned and strolled down the duckboards, his spurs ringing musically, headed toward Tomas's livery barn.

Constable Elmore watched him go with a speculative look on his face. Neither the constable, nor Jim Travis, saw the two other watchers. One was a girl, leaning against the grimy doorway to the blacksmith shop. Her face was intent, and just a bit admiring. The other was Brade Ballard, slouched in a chair by the window of the Anglica Saloon, peering past the many flyspecks thoughtfully. Brade finally left off staring at the man Elmore had told him was a Ranger, and looked over at the girl, his black eyes thoughtful.

IV

Gordo Tomas saddled the livery horse with mild curiosity. The same horse every time—but Gordo said nothing. He just smiled and nodded as Travis swung up, reined around, and rode out of town, northeast, over the shimmering land, then went back to his shady little office and drowsed. In fact, Gordo slept all through the coming and going of Brade Ballard, who coursed the stalls, saw which horse was gone, then walked back up the duck-boards, behind the constable's office, and soon rode down through town himself. Heading northeast, too.

Frank Liddell's deep eyes hooded their depths and hid the look behind a smile as he talked with Linda Barbera. He had pressed his suit as far as he dared. Now it was up to the girl either to discourage him, or encourage him, and so far she had done neither. He looked past and saw the rider she was watching. "Who is he?"

"A Ranger, Frank."

Liddell's smile fell apart; a rigid look crept up and puckered his face. "Oh? How do you know?"

"He was at the ranch last night." She didn't say how Jim had been rifle-herded by herself. "He wanted permission to trespass on War Bonnet."

"Why?"

Linda felt, more than saw, the vivid interest. It

made her uneasy in a tiny way. She shrugged. "He's looking for smugglers."

Liddell's eyes flickered, then he levered up the smile again and nodded to her. "Well, it looks like he's trespassing again, from the direction he rode out of Chiqui."

She scowled a little. "He'd better not. He's been warned."

Frank shrugged and started past her. "Well, got to get back to the store. Anyway, what's one trespasser? See you later, honey."

Linda nodded without speaking. Her eyes were pensive. She scarcely heard the merchant's words as her eyes caught the powerful, broad figure of another horseman riding northeast, out of town. She looked twice, then her eyes widened and the full underlip was caught harshly between her teeth. Recognition and disbelief—and something close to horror—flashed for a second as she stood rigidly and watched the second man ride out of sight.

Liddell never looked back. Only the blacksmith frowned when he had to tell Linda for the third time that her horse was ready. When she heard, she paid him quickly, swung up and heeled the animal suddenly and roared out of town, swung west, and disappeared over the cringing, heat-drowned War Bonnet range. The blacksmith reached up and scratched his head, then wagged it back and forth in pure wonder.

When the War Bonnet riders walked their horses evenly down the crooked roadway of Chiqui, the loungers scented trouble. Word went around that old Samuel Barbera himself was leading them, and that Jack Talbert wasn't along. Barbera swung down in front of the bank and went in, but the cowboys rode on over to the Anglica before they tied up. Barbera had ordered it that way; the bank's manager was his thumb stamp. Orders for Chiqui came through him. Barbera didn't condescend to issue ultimatums except through others. It was a part of his successful strategy. The banker's word was backed with Barbera's wealth, plus the bank's prestige. He went into the little cubbyhole office and dropped into a chair, and asked about this Ranger. Chiqui's bank was his clearing-house of information, and never failed him. He listened to everything the manager had picked up with his aloof, mahogany face set and wooden, and his frozen-steel eyes hooded and emotionless.

When Linda got home, the War Bonnet was almost deserted. There were only three people in the house. Herself, her mother, and a Mexican house girl. She sat down in the large parlor and wondered how to phrase her discovery, then plunged into it without further thought. Her mother's black eyes were liquidly intent. She sensed something. "He's back, Mother."

For a long time there was silence, then the older woman nodded slightly. "I knew it." She smiled and rocked gently. "He had to come."

"But why now? After seven years?"

The mother almost smiled. *"¿Quién sabe?"* A flicker of doubt darted over the black eyes. "Are you sure?"

"Yes. He's heavier, and a lot sterner-looking, in the face, and now he carries two guns. But it's Brade, Mother. I'd know him anywhere. Even after seven years."

The older woman smiled fully then, nostalgically. "He's three years older than you are, honey. Still, the pull of the blood is strong. You should know if it's your brother or not."

Linda got up with a frown. "Well, it was, all right, I know that."

"Where are you going?"

Linda's black eyes shone with perplexity. "I'm going to ride a little, Mother. I've got a feeling. . . ." She shrugged. "I don't know. For two days now I've been restless . . . uneasy. I'm going to ride around and see if I can't figure things out."

Her mother was looking up at her, wide-eyed. "You've been uneasy since the Ranger came, is that it?" She saw the color mount in her daughter's face and shrugged. "Well, then, go take your ride. Jack is riding, too."

Linda's frown deepened. "But I thought Dad said they were going into Chiqui."

"The boys went with your father. Jack said he wanted to do some riding. He said he'd heard there were more trespassers."

"Oh." The uneasiness became almost tangible. Linda threw a flashing smile to her mother and went back out into the blazing daylight. There was that odd sensation in her, stronger now. She mounted her horse, still puzzling over it, and the return to Chiqui of her brother, Brade Barbera, after his silent, seven-year absence. She knew by instinct that trouble was building up for the mighty War Bonnet.

Jim Travis saw the old ranch from the poop of his rented horse and sat back in the shaggy eminence of a juniper, studying it. There were wagon ruts leading to it, and a lot of saddle horse tracks going and coming, but, aside from those things it looked like hundreds of other discouraged, haunted old ruins throughout the cow country. He ran his fingers through the rank mane of the livery horse, sighed, and swung down. It took only a moment to loop the reins, turn the horse, and start him back toward Chiqui. Then he slipped forward afoot, got to the moldy-smelling old barn, whistled noiselessly at the amount of good hay and grain stored in it, and laboriously crawled into the ancient mow, where dust was decades thick. He lay down and waited.

The interior of the barn was like a blast furnace under the cracked and flapping roof slats. He sweated and found himself thinking of the black-eyed girl. It was a pleasant way to kill the hours until the burros came—if they came.

Jack Talbert rode into Chiqui not more than a half an hour after Samuel Barbera had left it. He had been watching from the covert. When War Bonnet rode out, he rode in, tied up in front of the Anglica, swung down, and walked jinglingly down to Liddell's Emporium.

Liddell looked up from a ledger, jerked his head toward a chair, and made a wry face. "Ranger snoopin' around."

"I figured that's who he was. But who'n hell's the other one?"

"What other one?" Liddell's face was tight again, wary and angry both.

Talbert rolled a cigarette. "I never seen him. The boys told me he backed up the Ranger's play when I got knocked out last night."

Frank Liddell sat perfectly still for a long moment, looking at Talbert. He didn't speak until after the foreman's cigarette was a smoking ember, then he shrugged.

"Didn't know there was but one. Maybe just a cowboy that didn't like the idea of War Bonnet ganging up on the damned Ranger."

"Yeah," Talbert agreed dryly. "An' maybe somethin' else, too."

"Like what?"

"Another Ranger."

Liddell nodded. "That's possible. After I discovered from Linda this other one was a Ranger, I went over and talked to Elmore."

"What'd he say?"

Liddell's eyes clouded in annoyance. "Nothing. Closed-mouthed old goat. He just gave me that wide-eyed look of his and said . . . 'Is that so? I hadn't heard.'"

Talbert's eyes darkened. "I don't like it, Frank. Rangers are bad medicine."

Liddell nodded speculatively. "Yeah. I watched him ride off northeast, too, Jack." He watched for the reaction and saw it immediately. Talbert's face swung toward him with a frozen look of wonder. The cigarette dangled forgotten.

"Toward the old barn, Frank?" It came out softly, guardedly.

Liddell nodded, still watching the War Bonnet foreman.

Talbert swore and got up. "I don't dare use the ranch riders on him if he's at the old place. Hell, they'd get suspicious, seein' the hay an' grain in there."

Still Liddell said nothing. He watched the seed of doubt he'd planted grow and develop in Talbert's less shrewd mind. Waiting for the total he knew was coming, because he knew Jack Talbert. He wasn't disappointed. "By gawd, I'll have to do this job myself. If he's snoopin' around out there." He looked down at Liddell. "Frank, we'd better quit . . . for a while, anyway. Rangers'd raise hell with both of us."

Liddell nodded thoughtfully and spoke then: "Yeah. After this shipment tonight, I'll pass word down the line. No more until we get a new receiving point." He reached up and knuckled one deep-set eye. "It's too bad, Jack. You keeping the old man stirred up on that no trespassin' hobby of his has made the War Bonnet the best damned depot in the Chiqui." He swore with irritation. "Well, we've made enough so's we can afford to lie back an' wait until things're ready again, huh?"

Talbert's baleful face sagged noticeably. "Maybe *you* have, Frank. I don't have much of it, any more."

Liddell nodded slightly; he knew his man. Jack Talbert could have $100,000 and he wouldn't have it long. He felt contempt for the lean, brutal man before him, but didn't let it show. Still, he couldn't resist one little barb. "Well, you sure got rid of Brade easy enough. Seven years, Jack. He's probably dead by now, as quick-tempered as he was."

Talbert's face stiffened. "He asked for it. Always taggin' after me and pryin', and double-checkin' the damned range tally sheets and askin' about the cattle that vanished." Jack's mind found satisfaction in the past that offset the uneasiness of the present and dwelt on Brade's banishment from the War Bonnet. He was even smiling a little. "Sam'l's a hot-headed old fool, too, or it wouldn't have worked." He half smiled and stamped out the cigarette on the office floor. "It wasn't hard to decoy Brade into an argument with Sam'l about the missing cattle. Brade accused Sam'l of not keeping enough outriders on the back country range, an' Sam'l accused Brade of knowing something about the vanished cattle. It was pretty good, at that. Sam'l swore an' cussed an' asked Brade how he knew how many riders were at the line camps, unless he'd slipped around on the out range, where he had no business. It was the same as sayin' Brade stole them damned critters himself. If I hadn't stepped in between them, then an' there, there'd've been blood." Jack laughed. "Steppin' in an' takin' Sam'l's part was the best thing I ever did. He made me foreman. A job for life." Talbert looked down at Frank Liddell. "It's paid off, too, Frank. Up to now."

Liddell turned impatiently back to his ledger with a stiff little smile. "It will again, Jack, just be patient. If it isn't gold, it'll be cattle again."

"Yeah. How about the Ranger, though, an' this other *hombre?*"

Frank looked up. "Forget the other man. He's just a coincidence. The Ranger, though, we'll have to discourage by stoppin' all packs after tonight." He looked back at the ledger. "That's all, Jack."

Talbert got the hint, shrugged, and walked out, still frowning. He knew Liddell would be at the deserted ranch on time. That was one good feature about Frank. He was always on time. Talbert turned on the duckboards and started back up toward his horse; there was a hard smile on his mouth. Why shouldn't Frank be on time? He'd always gotten plenty of money out of their dealings. In fact, he now had a flourishing store, built from the illegal fortune he'd made in smuggled gold and rustled cattle. Jack untied and swung up. And he had nothing to show for his share, but legendary gambling losses. He squirmed uncomfortably under the fierce heat and reined broodingly out of Chiqui.

V

Brade Ballard heard Talbert's horse coming over the still, breathless land, long before he saw the rider. He rode farther off into the distance, dismounted, tied up, and went back. He wasn't 100 feet away when the War Bonnet foreman went by. There was a savage, bitter light in the black eyes, but he didn't move until Talbert had ridden into the old barn and swung down. Then he went closer, hunkered in a trace work of manzanita shade, and waited with the stoic patience of his kind. There wasn't much to see, except when Jack grunted and forked the hay into the manger and dumped vast amounts of grain into the bunkers.

The dark eyes glinted softly. He watched Talbert's red face drip sweat from the exertion. Even with the sun sliding toward the sawtooths on the horizon, it was still insufferably hot. To Talbert and the Ranger in the stifling haymow, but not so unbearable to Brade Ballard—who had all but forgotten his other name, the right name of Barbera—because he felt the dying fires of a seven-year hate, and it cooled him.

Linda rode without aim or purpose. The feeling of impending disaster rode with her. She went eastward beyond Chiqui. She had intended to ride into town, but remembering that her father was there with the War Bonnet crew deterred her. Instead, she rode past the town, then swung northward so as to come onto the juniper and Digger pine section of the range where she could find shade and seclusion, since the section was never used for the cattle, unless riders were kept there, because of strays drifting over into Mexico, thus becoming lost to the War Bonnet.

When Jack Talbert finished putting out the feed, he carefully walked all around the old buildings, eyes squinted at the ground, looking for tracks of the Ranger that Frank Liddell had said rode out of Chiqui, northeastward. It was impossible to read much on the granite hard earth, in the maze of tracks from other days, so he finally contented himself with sitting in the shade of the old barn, squint-eyed and glaring over the shimmering land for sign of movement. Brade Ballard saw this and grew wary. He knew that something had alarmed Talbert. Sweat lay under his shirt and dried with a sticky sense of coolness. He didn't move. Didn't dare. Not until Talbert had smoked a cigarette and shrugged, then went back into the shade. Then Brade took his spurs off and walked back to his horse, narrow-eyed. Evidently Talbert thought the Ranger either hadn't found the old ranch, or hadn't arrived yet. If he'd thought otherwise, he'd have looked more closely.

Brade was swinging up when he heard a shod horse's hoof strike stone. It was a small sound, but distinct in the sharp, arid air. He went off again, listening. The sound came back to him. He waited motionlessly, one hand near his horse's nose to squeeze off any sound. When he saw Linda ride by, head down and lost in her thoughts, he was tempted to speak, to signal or step out. She was going directly toward the old ranch. He hesitated, confused, and by then she was close enough for the sound of her coming to carry to Jack Talbert. Brade left his horse and slipped forward again.

Linda saw the blackish old ruins ahead of her and vaguely remembered they had been erected by an early homesteader who her father had discouraged. She glanced at them indifferently and was reining around, when a voice slapped her to sudden, jarring reality and she reined back, stopping. "Hold it!"

The black eyes swept around and found the cold muzzle of a six-gun staring back. Behind the gun was Jack Talbert's sweaty, surprised face. For a long second neither spoke, then Talbert let the gun droop and flushed a raging crimson. "Linda! What in hell're you doing over here?"

His anger stung her to instant resentment. There had never been anything but shielded animosity between them, anyway. "Riding. What difference does it make?" She looked beyond him, saw the telltale glitter of sunlight on another pistol barrel. Unknowingly her eyes widened. Jack Talbert saw it, cursed, and spun around, but the range was empty. Fear mounted in him, the uneasiness was gone now, as were the rancor and dissatisfaction. Fear replaced both. He was wide-eyed when he motioned with the gun. "Ride over to the old barn." He started toward the building.

Linda glared. "Suppose I don't want to?"

He swung back and raised the gun again. "Then you'll damned well lie right where you are." She saw the wild fury in his eyes. The gun jerked quickly. "Move!"

Linda's small anger turned to amazement, then

seeping, growing fear. She reined toward the barn, rode inside, saw Talbert's horse inside, drowsing in the shade, and swung down at his order. For a while there was silence. Jack's face was pale under the red heat rash of perspiration; his eyes were dangerously thoughtful.

"Who'd you ride over here with?"

"No one. What's the matter with you?"

His anger flared. She'd unconsciously touched him on ragged nerves. He shook his head quickly, brusquely. "Nothing, not a damned thing. Where's that damned Ranger you brought to the house?" He didn't wait for an answer. His eyes widened a little as a thought struck him. "That was a put-up job, wasn't it? It didn't stick, though, did it?"

Linda was frowning. "What're you talking about?"

"You said you found him out on the range and herded him in with your rifle. Hell, I can see through that. You was meetin' him all the time. You brought him in to tell Sam'l about the smugglin'. Damn you, Linda, you're in this thing hand and glove with him, aren't you?"

The black eyes were wide. She was facing death and knew it. Also, she suddenly felt the unrest crystallize, a lot of other little facets dropped into place then, too, like Talbert's constant abuse of trespassers, and the way he kept her father stirred up. Dimly she remembered how Jack had sided against Brade. It all began to make a design she could understand.

"Jack, you're in that smuggling some way. I know it."

He slid his gun back into its holster with a hard smile. "Yeah? How'd ya know it?"

"I . . . I . . . can sense it. You're behind it, some way. Call it intuition, but I know it."

He nodded slowly. "Call it what you like, Linda. You're not going to talk much about it around Chiqui, or the War Bonnet. That's a promise." He was looking at her as something suddenly attainable. "Over the line's Mexico, Linda. You an' I're going over there after the burros come back. This time I'll take *all* the gold. Frank can rage all he wants to. I know when it's over. Besides, he don't need it like I do. I'll take it all, an' you, too."

Linda felt almost chilly. It was like a breath of doom, clammy and cold, had suddenly blown over her. She watched Talbert nodding his head with that awful, tight smile, and could feel the words dying in her throat. Then she heard another voice. It was soft and clear, like a bell, with a bell's impersonal detachment, and she recognized it in spite of its acquired knife edge and timbre. Her brother's voice, Brade Barbera. "Jack, turn around."

Talbert started suddenly, then froze. His eyes were fixed intently on Linda. She could see the parade of thoughts that flashed over them. He made no move to obey and she heard the voice again, coming from the sun-bleached yard just beyond the barn's maw.

"Turn, Jack. You've given the orders long enough. Turn now, and take an order. Just one, Jack. Turn!"

There could be no mistaking the deadliness of that command. It rang like a knell. When the War Bonnet foreman turned, someone was going to die.

Talbert's wild eyes narrowed, contracted, and seemed to grow opaque and glassy. Linda watched from off to one side with fascination. Talbert turned slowly, very slowly, keeping his gun hand free, but away from the pistol butt that hung so comfortingly, so accessibly at his hip, then he sucked in his breath and Linda tore her eyes off him and looked at the wide-legged man, leaning forward a little, motionless and beady-eyed, in the glare of the sunlight. Talbert breathed a name, almost hoarsely: "Brade."

The two-gun man nodded with one small movement of his head. "Yeah. Brade Barbera. It used to be that, Jack. Now it's Brade Ballard." The long beak of a nose, thin and dark and slightly hooked, showed outside of the perimeter of the man's hat brim of shade. "Seven years, Jack. I didn't find out about you an' Frank Liddell until two months ago. Talbert, Liddell, an' old Epifanio Escalante, down at Fronteras. You three been damned good, up until now, Jack. First War Bonnet cattle, then this gold smugglin' deal. Maybe I'd've never found it out, Jack, except I went down to see my wife's folks at Fronteras. They knew all about it. The gold I could overlook, Jack, but not the War Bonnet cattle ... or the way you've always worked to turn my dad against me." The black eyes never left Talbert's flushed, shiny face. "Linda, move away from him."

She was starting to obey when another voice cut in. Linda and Brade started, but Brade's face pulled into a faint, sardonic smile. "Hold on, down there. Don't any of you make a move." There was a scramble, then a *thud* behind them, and Jim Travis walked stiffly out of the shadows, his clothes streaked with dust and dried sweat. There was the small, glistening brilliance of his badge, high on his shirt. He was moving with open authority; there was no longer any need for secrecy. He disarmed Jack Talbert with one muscular swoop, then nodded at Brade. "Chuck it, *hombre*."

Brade holstered his guns, straightened with a hard, granite smile at Talbert, and walked into the shade of the old barn as Jim Travis smiled uncertainly at Linda, then turned toward the men.

"Talbert, I can't recall ever nabbin' a man I disliked as much as I dislike you." He turned toward Brade. "Who're you, *hombre?*"

Brade mopped at his dark forehead. "I'm the *hombre* who packed your saddle into Chiqui the morning Talbert here had your horse shot out from under you. I been watchin' you ever since you hit Chiqui. Y'see, when I found out what Talbert was doin' . . . through my wife's kinsmen down at Fronteras, in old Mexico . . . I wrote to the Texas Rangers and gave 'em all the dope I had. Then I rode on into Chiqui myself, to sort of be on hand, should the Ranger they sent need any help" Brade nodded toward the haymow. "I followed you like a shadow, pardner. In fact, I saw you go up there an' been waitin' outside ever since." He smiled widely at Linda. Brade's smile was a flashing, brilliant thing that completely altered his face. "Hi, Sis," he said.

Linda walked over with a funny little, half-tearful look that wasn't quite a smile or a sob. "I'm awfully glad you're back, Brade. Mother will be, too."

His smile went flat. "Dad, too, Sis?" She knew what he meant and didn't answer. Quickly he reached over, took her hand, and squeezed it. "Don't worry, Linda, honey. We'll see what happens before we judge the old cuss. I don't really hold it against him an' you, and Mom shouldn't. It's the way he had to keep above water here, in the Chiqui, in his day." He turned back to Jim with a self-conscious smile. "Now what, Ranger?"

"Get to horse an' ride for town."

Brade nodded softly. "All right. I caught that horse you turned loose an' tied him up. Let's go."

Jim let Brade watch the crestfallen, sullen foreman of the War Bonnet while he maneuvered Linda
Barbera up ahead of him. For a long time they rode
along engulfed in their own thoughts and the sudden unmasking of the smuggling plot under the
very nose of the Barbera clan, then Linda looked
over at Jim Travis. Her eyes flickered from the small,
burnished badge, glittering harshly under the merciless sun, to his rugged, honest face, and she blushed
because her thoughts were not bitter, as they once
had been. Jim looked down, caught her looking. She
had to say something quick, to cover up her embarrassment. The blush remained, however. "Did you
know Frank Liddell was mixed up in it, too?"

Jim shook his head. "No, not exactly. I sort of wondered about him, but until I heard your brother say
what he knew, I wasn't more than just suspicious."
He studied her handsome profile somberly. Brade
saw the look and stared in surprise. He'd had no
idea—he shrugged. It happens once to everyone. He
turned and glared at Talbert and didn't hear Jim's
words.

"Linda?"

"Yes?"

Their eyes were locked, shy yet challenging. Both
were dusky with high color. "Do . . . do . . . you really think I'm as ornery as you made me think in
town, there by the blacksmith shop?"

She let her eyes drop before his glance, and shook
her head. "No. It was just that . . . well . . . like you
said once . . . we, on the War Bonnet, have trouble
on the inside. In the family."

Jim nodded. "Brade?"

"Yes. He an' Dad had an. . . ."

"Well, pretty quick you'll have the answer to that, honey."

She looked up at the interruption. Ranger Travis was looking straight ahead and pointing. They saw the riders coming toward them over the wavy land, reined up, and waited. Linda nodded without speaking. It was her father with the War Bonnet cowboys. No one spoke until Samuel Barbera reined up, his hard-eyed riders at his back, and let his cold eyes range over them. They stopped dead still at the sight of Brade. Tension was in the air like electricity. Jim Travis looked among the War Bonnet men for the wispy rider who had shot his horse out from under him. The man wasn't there.

He turned a thin mouth and bitter eye on Barbera and spoke, yanking the man's glance from Brade. "I told you about the smugglers, Barbera, an' I've got one." He wagged his head to Talbert. "Now, if you'll get out of the way, I'll go get the other one."

Barbera acted as if he hadn't heard. His eyes fell on Linda, beside the badge-wearing Ranger. He seemed lost in thought, and, when he spoke, it startled all of them. He swept the cold blue eyes past Travis. "You back to stay, Brade?"

The hawk-faced son squinted, saw the pleading, poignant look in his sister's face as she twisted in the saddle, looking at him. He shrugged. "I reckon. Why?"

Barbera's face didn't yield, but his voice was husky. "Glad to have you back, Son."

Travis nudged the girl. "Come on, Linda, let's go get Frank Liddell. It'll make me feel good to nab him with you as bait." His eyes were grinning wickedly down at her.

She flashed him a warm glance. "Aren't you afraid of being baited, too, Mister Ranger?"

"No'm. I'm just a willing sucker." They blushed, laughed, and rode off.

Barbera's massive hand engulfed his son's harder, leaner hand. Peace had come to the War Bonnet.

Halfmoon Ranch

I

Alturas lay in the Washoe Valley, a part of Nevada where for nine months out of each year the land lay sere and dusty from lack of rain. As cow towns went, Alturas was typical; it had been thrown together by men in a hurry. Its buildings were for the most part unpainted, weathered, and warped. It was an ugly place except perhaps at sunrise and sunset when quiet shadows softened its sharp corners, its rough planking, and its scuffed boardwalks.

But notwithstanding its functional ugliness Alturas was a thrifty town. Cowmen for miles around did their buying here as well as their banking. The Alturas *Clarion*, owned and operated by John Arnold, had often made the point editorially that if a grubby little tent town called Reno was richer, this was only a transitory affair because cattle were the mainstay of Nevada's commerce while gold mining had always in the past, in Nevada, California, or elsewhere, proven a will-o'-the-wisp.

Everyone in Alturas agreed with John about this. Generally they agreed with him on other matters he editorialized about, too, such as the caustic comments he had to make about the advent of the notorious gunman, Mike Ayers, when Ayers and an unknown companion rode into Alturas.

But John Arnold, who'd matured in a lawless land, was far too cagey to mention Ayers by name. What he said in his *Clarion* editorial was that the

Washoe Valley had survived flash floods, Paiute war parties, highwaymen, and Mormon missionaries, and did not now need professional gunmen to aid it in keeping the peace or promoting beef sales.

Folks knew who John meant and they slyly smiled. Even Sheriff Lew Burton, normally a taciturn, wry man, got a chuckle out of that editorial. But Ed Grosson, president of the Alturas Drovers & Merchants Bank, didn't. Ed told Lew he thought someone ought to put a muzzle on John Arnold, that all he ever did was stir things up.

They were in Ed's office with its green shades and its green-painted plank floor when Ed told Lew Burton that. Ed slapped the newspaper on his desk like it was an annoying child.

"Gunfighters have passed through Alturas before!" he exclaimed pithily. "The best course is to let 'em pass along. This . . . this stupid editorial is the kind of thing that could irritate a man with Ayers's reputation, which could mean trouble. What's the point of it, Lew, what difference does it make that Ayers is here?"

"Maybe no difference," agreed burly, graying Lew Burton, still with a dry twinkle in his eye. "Maybe he's just passing through, as you say, Ed. But in case he's not, in case he's here for some purpose, that editorial will let him know how the wind's blowing in Alturas."

"Bunk," snorted portly, perpetually frowning Ed Grosson. "When I was a young man just starting out, I saw my share of those gunfighters, Lew. A thing like this doesn't bother them. If he's here for a purpose, he'll go about his business and someone's stupid editorial won't slow him down one bit. But it just might make him mad enough to tree the town. I tell you, Lew, someone ought to muzzle John Arnold. He's nothing but a busybody. He doesn't print news. He prints scurrilous gossip."

Lew left Grosson's office with a puckish little smile down around his lips. He'd been a peace officer in Washoe County twenty years. He knew the people of his territory and he also knew the gossip. He could distinctly remember, fifteen years back, another of Arnold's biting editorials. That time it had been about a local banker and a woman named Clarissa Benton. Clarissa had come to Alturas on the westbound stage. She'd stayed in town four months and in that time Ed Grosson's wife's brothers had threatened to horsewhip Ed and ride Clarissa out of town on a rail. They'd never had to do either; one day Clarissa boarded the stage and no one ever saw her again.

A few old-timers still remembered that passionate affair and, like Lew Burton, they'd slyly wink and slyly smile whenever they heard Ed rant and rave against John Arnold. Ed Grosson had a long memory and a vindictive one, but he was transparent to the old-timers who remembered things from fifteen years back.

Lew crossed from the bank side of the dusty roadway to his combination office and jail. It was cool morning now but in another couple of hours the bitter summer sun would turn pale and fierce. He had a drunk Mexican to release and some Wanted posters to sort through, but, aside from that, things were quiet enough. Ordinarily in midsummer Washoe Valley was orderly enough; it got just too cussed hot for enterprising outlaws to stir, it seemed. At least that's the way Lew Burton interpreted the drop-off in crime throughout his bailiwick during the midsummers, and he'd been enforcing the law in Washoe County long enough to know.

Amos Darren came in just as Lew was turning out that Mexican with the throbbing head. Amos was a big, light-complexioned man with china blue eyes and a granite chin. It had been in his establishment, Darren's Bar, that the *vaquero* had gotten troublesome the night before, so big Amos put his stony gaze upon the Mexican and silently waited until Lew gave his prisoner back his gun, his boot knife, his crumpled paper money, and threw in a strong brief lecture to boot, then discharged the cowboy. After that Amos and Lew were alone in the office. Lew looked mildly at the larger man, saying nothing. He knew Darren for a man who spoke out when he had something to say, so he waited.

"Have you seen John's editorial?" the saloon man asked, looking annoyed. "Lew, that Ayers feller was in my place when his sidekick came in with a copy of the paper. Ayers read it and made some pretty pointed remarks."

Lew still stood there, saying nothing. There would be more to come. He knew Amos Darren that well.

"What's the matter with that damned Arnold anyway? Why's he always trying to stir up a fuss?"

Lew sat down, thumbed back his hat, and blew out a long breath. "John's a believer in free speech, no matter where it takes him. You know that, Amos. You've been in Alturas six years now. You've seen him do this before when something came up he thought needed airing."

"Sure. Who cares about a little gossip, but this could be different. You get one of those men like Mike Ayers on his ear about something and you've got real trouble. I just don't see any benefit coming out of writing junk like that an' I think you ought to go take John to task a little."

Sheriff Burton shook his head. His expression was wry. "He's broken no law, except perhaps the law of caution, and, as far as I know, that's not even a misdemeanor, let alone a felony. I can't do anything, Amos. Anyway, I think you and Ed Grosson are makin' a mountain out of a molehill. Ayers is just passing through more'n likely. There's nothing here for him. The valley's peaceful and the town's swelterin' out another blisterin' summer. No one's spoilin' for trouble that I've heard of."

Big Amos stood there, gazing downward. He was privately making an assessment. Lewis Burton was nearing fifty. He looked tough and capable enough, but he talked like a tired old man. Perhaps it was time someone younger replaced him. Amos was on the town council along with Ed Grosson and a couple of other local men. He was thinking perhaps this ought to be brought up at the next council sitting. Maybe Lew could be induced to retire.

"The trouble with restricting folks," said Lew as he tilted back his chair, "is that you can't limit it once you start it. There's the Women's League. You know how they feel about your saloon, Amos. Restrict John Arnold, muzzle a few others, curtail this place or that place, and the next thing you know the ladies'll be in here swearing out warrants to have your bar closed. You can be with freedom or you can be without it, but no one's figured out how you can have it and not have it at the same time."

"All right," retorted Darren. "But what about Ayers and his sidekick?"

"What about 'em? Have they hurt you? No. And they haven't hurt anyone else, either." Lew squinted his gray, steady eyes at the big man across from him. "You know how to avoid trouble, Amos?" he asked. "I'll tell you how . . . don't go lookin' for it where it doesn't exist, until you start proddin' it to life."

"Lew, you didn't hear what Ayers said about that silly editorial. He was pretty burned up about what John had written."

"I expect," said Burton calmly, "every gunfighter like Mike Ayers has read worse things about himself in newspapers many times. I don't recollect hearing that the mortality rate among writers like John is near as high as it is among saloon men, for instance." Burton tipped down his chair, riffled through papers on his desk, and dropped his gaze. It was a clear indication of dismissal and Amos took it this way. He went over to the door, abruptly halted there, looking out, and said softly over his shoulder: "Lew, you're about to have company. It's Mike Ayers himself." Then Amos stepped out and went walking southward.

Burton was watching the door, his face carefully expressionless, his shrewd, dead-level eyes thoughtful and interested when the gunfighter stepped up, hesitated a moment, then passed on over the threshold.

Ayers was not particularly tall yet he gave that impression because he carried no spare flesh on his bones. He was a leaned-down, tough, and durable man with a long mouth, liquid large eyes, and a variety of complete assurance that preceded him wherever he went. He was, Lew thought, in his late twenties or early thirties. He moved with a deceptive deliberateness, never fast but without ever turning left when he should turn right.

He was known in six Western states as one of the deadliest men with a gun alive, yet he had not, to Lew Burton's knowledge, ever actually been an outlaw. There were rumors and legends galore about Mike Ayers; some said he was a merciless killer, while others said he was a sort of Robin Hood. Lew shrewdly figured the actual truth was somewhere in between, and Lew was a pretty fair judge of men.

But until this morning he'd never before laid eyes on Mike Ayers, so he made a careful appraisal as Ayers passed over to his desk. Ayers was a handsome man; there was no getting around that. His features were good; he entirely lacked coarseness, and he had a wide-shouldered, narrow-hipped, lithe kind of grace that set him apart. His clothing was clean, too, which was unusual in a land where most men were bachelors and were ordinarily none too careful about their attire.

For some inexplicable reason Ayers put Lew Burton in mind of an old cowman who'd recently died up in the Horseshoe Hills north of town, old Pete Frazier. Pete had been built like that, lean and not really tall although giving that impression. And old Pete had been one of those clean men; in fact, it had been a joke at the cow camps how old Pete went to town every Friday in his rig for his laundry at the Chinaman's place. But that wasn't entirely it, either. There was something else about those two that made Lew think of Frazier while looking at Mike Ayers, although he just couldn't put his finger on it.

Ayers pushed out a hand, said his name, and, when Burton shook with him, Ayers faintly smiled as though there was something about this handshake that secretly amused him. Lew dropped Ayers's hand, motioned for the gunfighter to be seated, and swung around to watch Ayers draw up a slat-bottomed chair and drop down in it, push out his long legs, and turn all loose and comfortable in the office hush and coolness. Lew sat there, waiting. He was a taciturn man. When others visited his office, he let them speak first. It was a longstanding rule of his to let visitors let off steam before speaking. This time, he told himself, he'd be earnestly told what kind of a scoundrel John Arnold was, and, if John ever printed another editorial like that again, Ayers would overhaul John's carcass, or something to that effect.

But Lew was wrong. He knew it the minute Ayers began speaking. The gunfighter's voice was quiet, well-modulated, almost drawling. He wasn't angry; he wasn't even outwardly annoyed.

"I reckon you read what it said about me in the *Clarion*, Sheriff. No names were mentioned, but the article was plain enough."

Lew nodded. "I heard about it," he said.

Ayers thinly smiled, his calm gaze unwaveringly upon Lew. "Well, maybe it's characteristic of folks that they jump to conclusions. Anyway, that writer is sure entitled to his opinion. We wouldn't deny that, would we, Sheriff?"

"No."

"But he was wrong in most of the things he said, Sheriff. At least I think he was, and I think something else, too. I think he's going to eat those words."

Lew's lids drooped a little. His mouth drew inward slightly, flattening against his teeth in an unpleasant way. Ayers noticed this craggy expression and gently shook his head.

"No trouble," he said. "Not like you're thinking,

Sheriff. Sure, it stung a little when I first read that editorial. But I'm not going after this Arnold feller. I'm going to let him come after me."

"Oh?" said Lew. "What's that mean, Mister Ayers?"

"I'm settling hereabouts, Sheriff. I'm going to let Arnold keep his eye on me, and maybe in a year or so when he's satisfied he was wrong in saying Washoe Valley doesn't want my kind . . . that is, if he's man enough to admit a mistake when he makes one . . . I'll be waiting for him to apologize. Not in words, Sheriff, in print. Apologize in print just like he defamed me in print."

Lew pursed his lips. He let all that pass about John Arnold; it didn't interest him. What held his undivided attention now was what Mike Ayers had said about settling in the Washoe country.

"You figurin' on openin' a business, Mister Ayers?"

"No." The gunfighter drew forth a long white envelope and handed it to Sheriff Burton. "That's the deed to thirty-eight hundred acres of land in the Horseshoe Hills, Sheriff. There's also a deed in there to six hundred head of cattle branded with my uncle's Halfmoon mark."

Lew Burton's eyes flew wide open. "Halfmoon . . . ? Are you telling me, Mister Ayers, that old Pete Frazier left you his ranch when he passed on?"

"I am, Sheriff. Pete Frazier was my mother's only brother. He was my uncle."

Lew dropped his gaze to the bulky envelope he was holding. He made no examination of the contents of that envelope but he was very conscious of the earlier mystery of the similarity between Ayers and old Pete Frazier that had struck him.

"Odd," he muttered, turning the envelope over

and over as though it were some strange type of missile. "Odd as the devil, Mister Ayers, but, when you walked in here, you put me in mind of old Pete. By golly, I couldn't say why that was at all."

"No great mystery, Sheriff. My mother used to tell me I was a ringer for her brother."

"Yeah," mumbled Lew, handing back the envelope. "Have you recorded those papers?"

"Yes, when I got into town."

"Been up to your uncle's ranch yet?"

"No. My pardner and I've been on the trail three weeks. We're sort of dehydrated from riding over deserts this time of year. There's no hurry anyway, is there?"

"None that I know of, Mister Ayers." Lew recovered from his astonishment. "Funny thing, I knew your uncle twenty years. In all that time I never heard him mention that he was related to you."

The lithe gunfighter stood up, pocketed his large envelope, and dryly said: "He probably had his reasons, Sheriff." He didn't elaborate on this, but Lew understood what he meant. Folks who had professional gunfighters in their family trees didn't ordinarily go around talking about it.

"Yeah," said Lew in the same dry way. He stood up and nodded as Mike Ayers passed toward the door on his way out of the jailhouse.

II

John Arnold was a short man, which was a little unusual because his daughter, Evelyn, was tall. They were unalike in other ways, too. John, for example, had light brown hair; at least it had once been light brown, but now it was gray and none too thick. Evelyn, on the other hand, had a kind of coppery-colored hair. Sometimes, in the evenings when a red sun was setting, her hair seemed almost blood-red and rusty. John was a vitriolic person and Evelyn was not this way at all. She was thoughtful, sometimes downright solemn, and she had a way of laying her gaze upon people in a way that could warm them or chill them to the bone.

She was, the old-timers said, almost a twin to the way her mother had looked twenty-five years before. But Evelyn's mother—John's wife—had been dead now nine years, leaving John in his daughter's care.

There had been plenty of panting cowboys and even townsmen come courting since Evelyn had grown to womanhood, but she'd never married, and, while this always troubled the local womenfolk, it did not appear to bother Evelyn at all. Most certainly it was the least of John's troubles; he hadn't yet met the man he thought was a suitable mate for his daughter, but there was nothing unusual about that attitude of a father toward his only child.

John's main source of friction with his fellowmen

was what he called his "duty." He had a nose for
news and an inherent urgency to print it and comment editorially upon it. This was, he'd been saying
for twenty years in his newspaper office, his "duty"
to the community. There had been times when John's
"duty" had come within an ace of getting his skull
cracked, but one thing about John Arnold everyone
agreed on—he was no coward.

He knew the minute he saw shambling Lew Burton approaching across the road through his print
shop window, what was coming, and from lifelong
habit he straightened his shoulders, hitched up his
pants, waited for the door to open, braced and ready
for the denunciation.

Lovely Evelyn, too, saw the sheriff approaching,
but her reaction was different; she had a strong feeling of affection for Lew Burton. He'd been more
than a friend to her since childhood. She'd found
him wise and tolerant and understanding. She'd often contrasted Burton and her father and Lew had
never come off second best, although it was a difficult comparison because those two were so entirely
different. Her father was peppery, caustic, often
opinionated, and sometimes as truculent as a banty
rooster, while Lew was none of these things. What
had never ceased to amaze Evelyn was how these
two so vastly different men had remained such
staunch friends all these years.

They argued endlessly; once or twice they'd even
stopped speaking for weeks at a time. But in the end
one or the other always managed to be casually
standing where the other was bound to appear, and
they'd gravely flip a coin to see which one bought
the coffee, neither one speaking throughout this rit-

ual, and afterward they'd enter a café or a bar shoulder to shoulder and that would be the end of that particular disagreement. If Evelyn had ever been forced to say which one she loved the most, it would have been a heart-rending decision to make, but she was a young woman and those two were middle-aged men, so this decision would never present itself; each could make little forays into the world of the other, but they could never remain there for long, for age is a barrier none can successfully abrogate for very long.

"It'll be the Ayers thing," growled John as Sheriff Burton paused outside, reaching for the latch. "Evvie, you stay out of it."

Evelyn was racking type with papers wrapped about her wrists. She looked around to catch sight of Sheriff Burton's expression before making up her mind to obey her father or not. Lew's expression was serene when he entered, so Evelyn smiled at him, turned back, and resumed her work, satisfied there wouldn't be any need for her to intercede between old friends.

John, standing beside his old desk, didn't give the sheriff a chance. He said straight out: "All right, I antagonized Mike Ayers. But what I said still goes. Washoe County doesn't want his type."

Lew strolled over, eased down upon the edge of John's desk with one booted foot dangling, and looked critically around. "It may not want him, John, but it's got him. Not for a few days, either . . . for as long as he wants to stay. He inherited old Pete Frazier's ranch and cattle."

"*What?*"

"That's the size of it, John. He's Pete's nephew."

John's squinted, feisty eyes sprang wide. His jaw sagged, and even Evelyn, standing over across the room, turned to put a long gaze upon the sheriff.

"He's old Frazier's nephew?" asked John, astonished. "Lew, are you sure of that? I never heard Pete mention any family."

Burton sat there distantly smiling as though something had just occurred to him. Eventually he said: "You know, now that I think back on it, I can see where this gave old Pete a chuckle. He was a cantankerous old cuss at times. I'll bet he died smiling, knowing folks' reaction when his heir rode into town. Pete was like that."

John Arnold sat down, put his hands upon the table, and studied their mottled backs. Lew got off the desk, gazed from Evelyn to her father, walked as far as the streetside door, and said: "Give him a chance, John. The same chance you'd give any other newcomer. Even without your editorials he's not going to have an easy time of it here. Folks never let one of those fellers live private . . . whatever they do, folks put the worst possible interpretation on it."

John said nothing, but Evelyn quietly nodded over at Lew, and, although she did not say anything, either, Lew understood that she would see to it that Mike Ayers had his chance, as far as the Alturas *Clarion* was concerned.

Lew left the newspaper office, crossed the road, and ran into Mike Ayers's partner, a stocky, powerfully muscled man with challenging eyes and a tough-set mouth. Lew said amiably: "You boys going to ride up to Halfmoon?"

Ayers's partner nodded while considering Lew Burton dispassionately. "Mike figures, if we leave town for a few days, it'll be best for all concerned.

We'll make a tally of the cattle and get familiar with the range boundaries."

Lew nodded. This made sense. He stood there a little longer, wondering about this stocky man. "Don't believe we've met," he said, and pushed out a hand. "I'm Lew Burton."

"Yeah, I know. I'm Smoky Buel. I'll be range boss for Mike."

As Lew dropped Buel's hand, he said: "You been with him long, Smoky?"

The cowman's gaze hardened a little against Lew; his expression showed that he resented this prying question. "Long enough, Sheriff. We grew up together. When he got word of the inheritance, he wired me to meet him at Cheyenne. We rode down here together. Anything else you want to know?"

Lew shook his head. He could feel the antagonism forming here and side-stepped it. "Nothing more, Smoky. I wouldn't have asked that, only after you boys ride out I'm going to be busy spikin' rumors that folks'll start hereabouts."

Buel's gaze softened a little. "I reckon you will, at that," he said dryly. "That's the hell of it. A feller's good with guns and folks make him out something other than what he is every time."

"That sounds about right. I've said it once before today and I'll say it again. It's not going to be easy for you two hereabouts. I hope you boys can cut the mustard."

Buel shortened the reins he was holding as though to continue on across the road. "We can cut it, Sheriff. All Mike wants is for folks to leave us alone. But if they got to make judgments, to do it on what we show ourselves to be, not on a lot of untrue stories they've heard."

"I think they will, Smoky. I know the people of Washoe County pretty well. They listen to gossip like everyone else does, but they don't usually make any snap judgments. Well, you boys know the way up to Halfmoon?"

"Yeah. Thanks, anyway, Sheriff."

Sure," said Lew, and watched Smoky Buel hike on over to the boarding house hitch rack and tie up there. He teetered upon the far gangplank's edge for a moment, thinking over what he'd said to Buel. He hadn't exaggerated; Washoe County wouldn't jump to any conclusions about Mike Ayers. There had been other gunmen pass through from time to time. Outside of perhaps John Arnold and one or two others, no one had made any big issue out of their presence.

Of course, this was a little different. Ayers was not just passing through. Still, if he didn't make trouble, it was very unlikely that any trouble would come.

The longer Lew stood there, the better he felt about all this. If Ayers and his *segundo* stayed up at Halfmoon a week or two, it would help folks either to forget his presence or accept it normally.

Lew entered his office, tossed down his hat, and went across to the potbellied little iron stove where he traditionally made himself a cup of coffee every day about this time. He had the fire crackling, the water set to boil, and was measuring out miserly spoonfuls of coffee when Ed Grosson walked in through the open door, mopped sweat from his face with a white handkerchief, and waited for Lew to finish his measuring.

"I just heard something," Grosson said finally. "Ayers inherited the Frazier outfit."

"It's true enough," replied Lew, capping his coffee jar and replacing it upon a shelf beside the stove. "Sit down, Ed. You look like the heat's about to get you."

"Not the heat . . . that damned rumor. Lew, did you check with the recorder to make certain Ayers isn't just running a boomer on us?"

"Not yet, but I'm going to."

Lew crossed to his desk, sank down there, and turned comfortably limp. Grosson looked troubled, so Lew did what he ordinarily did, he waited.

"I never heard Frazier had a nephew, Lew."

"Neither did I, but that doesn't mean anything. He wasn't the most talkative feller I ever knew."

Grosson finally sat down, put away his handkerchief, and scowled at the sheriff. "Eagleton won't like this, if it turns out to be legal."

"Cy Eagleton," said Burton, "can like it or lump it. If it turns out that Ayers has sound legal title, that's all there'll be to it, Ed."

"I doubt that, Lew. I doubt that like hell. Eagleton's been borrowing heavy from the bank to implement his expansion plans. Halfmoon's not only adjacent. It's the best parcel of open range in the Horseshoe Hills. He won't take it kindly, a stranger . . . and *what* a stranger . . . walking in and taking it over. You know how Eagleton is when he's upset, Lew."

Burton put his head to one side, listening to the coffee pot begin its merry sounds. "Seven minutes," he murmured. "You know, Ed, there's quite an art to making good coffee. Let it boil exactly seven minutes."

Grosson's gaze turned testy. "We were discussing Halfmoon, Ayers, and Eagleton . . . remember?"

"Sure I remember. I can sum up my thoughts on

that topic real easy. First off, if Ayers's title is good, he owns Halfmoon and that's all there is to that. Second, if Cyrus Eagleton wants Halfmoon, he'll have to buy it from Ayers. And third, Ed, Eagleton will be making one of the biggest mistakes of his life if he tries getting tough with Ayers and Buel. That's a pair a man would want to do a heap of serious thinkin' over, before he tried anything rough."

"Who's Buel?"

"Ayers's pardner and range boss. Smoky Buel. That feller who rode in with Ayers."

"Oh, yeah, that husky, craggy-looking man."

Lew got up. "Care for some coffee?" he asked.

Grosson also got up, but he shook his head. "It's a hundred and ten out and you want hot coffee." He made a snorting sound and stalked out of the jailhouse office.

Lew grinned, crossed to the stove, poured himself an enamelware cup of black brew, closed the damper, and took the coffee back to the desk with him. There, he lost his smile, turning grave and thoughtful.

III

Old Pete Frazier had grown up with Washoe County. He'd been one of the extremely few Gentiles accepted by a predominantly Mormon population in the early days, but he'd proven himself a hardworking, honest, and sincere neighbor, so the friction that had caused bad trouble and even bloodshed elsewhere had never come his way at all.

He had never married; his entire lifetime had been spent in putting together his Halfmoon outfit in the Horseshoe Hills. As Nevada spreads went, it was not a large ranch, but it was ample and prosperous, its cattle were the best selective breeding could produce, its water holes were year-around affairs, and its bottom land was as good as any in the territory.

In his sundown years old Pete had passed up many chances to sell out at a respectable profit, but, as he'd once said to Lew Burton, when a man hits seventy his needs are few, money's no longer important to him, and where else could he go and be happy. He knew every juniper tree, every rock and water hole of his Horseshoe Hills place, and no other spot on earth would ever be home to him.

His range had been carved out of an old Paiute *ranchería*. It was the best land for fifty miles in any direction. When others had to get 200 deeded acres to run one cow, old Pete's land would easily accommodate three times the critters he owned, but Pete had been a conservationist at heart; he was not the spoiler most cowmen were, and in this his thinking was sound. If fifty acres of land would accommodate two cows and a man ran only one cow on that fifty acres, then over the years his range would steadily improve so that, if one of those freak winters came with snowdrifts three feet high, his animals would survive where the cattle of his neighbor's would die by the hundreds.

Pete had made a lifelong ritual of riding his range, too. Because there were very few fences in Washoe County and also because the lush grasses on his land enticed every stray critter for 100 miles in every direction, he'd had to do that to preserve his graze. He'd never been disagreeable about it, though, had never ordered neighboring cattlemen to keep their critters away, for old Pete Frazier had been a cowman; he knew that without fences a man could not blame a dumb cow brute for following her nose to sweet water and green grass when her gut was shrunken from a steady diet of salt grass and alkali dust.

So old Pete had left behind a legacy that would have caused two-legged vultures to congregate in any cow country, and they congregated, too. He hadn't been a week in the summer-hard ground of the Alturas cemetery when bands of Flying E cattle were drifted over onto his land. These were gaunted cows tucked up from months of trying to eke out a survival existence on alkali and blessed little else. If the flies hadn't worried them to exhaustion, the dry water holes had. And if these two sources of anguish hadn't been enough to make bones stand straight up under shrunken hides, then the dearth of good grass was.

They fanned out over Halfmoon range mingling with Halfmoon critters, their contrasting gauntness immediately apparent to Smoky Buel when he and Mike Ayers rode along twin wagon ruts northward through the gentle hills to a weathered, hushed, and ancient set of ranch buildings set in a grove of huge old cottonwood trees, with a hollowed log running straight out of a hillside where water ran constantly into a huge, circular old wooden trough.

These buildings were gray from uncounted seasonal changes, first the biting cold of Nevada winters, then this searing, burning summertime heat. Where Mike drew rein with Smoky, there was also something else, a degree of deep solitude that was both sad and ghostly.

"Like the old man's still here," said Smoky, sitting up there studying how each outbuilding had been wisely set for access, for convenience and utility. "It makes a feller want to talk in a whisper. Mike, tell me something. How well did you know your uncle?"

"Not at all, Smoky. I met him only once, when he came north when I was a little kid. All I remember about him was that he was a quiet, rough-looking man who wore old-fashioned clothes but rode a mighty fine horse. After my mother died, I got a letter from him once. He sort of hinted that I might want to come down and live at Halfmoon with him." Ayers slackened his reins, swung down, and looked gravely ahead where the main ranch house stood. "I was pretty young and wild then. It never occurred to me that he was old and lonely. I didn't even answer the letter. Instead, I saddled up and went down to Arizona."

Smoky also dismounted. "I know how that is,"

he said, turning his back to Mike and tugging loose his *cincha*. "When a feller's young, he's pretty self-centered. When he's old enough to realize the important things, it's usually too late." Buel yanked down his saddle, dumped it in dust, and headed for a corral with his sweaty horse. Over his shoulder he said: "Leave yours. I'll take care of him while you're walkin' around, lookin' things over."

Mike twisted to watch Smoky walk off. How many range men would understand how it was with Mike at this quiet time, how he'd want to be alone for a little while? Not many. He turned back to facing forward again. There weren't very many like Smoky Buel in this life.

The stillness was depressing. Everywhere Mike strolled, he encountered reminders that another man's hand had labored here. That hollowed-out log carrying water to the trough, for instance. He stood by the trough, thinking how tedious it must have been to heat iron and burn that cored-out hollow from one end of the log to the other. A flash of bright color caught his attention and he looked down. There were plump goldfish in the trough. Now how, he marveled, had his uncle ever gotten those fish up into the Horseshoe Hills alive? Of course it could be done, but how many cattlemen thought that much of keeping their troughs clean of the green scum that ordinarily lined troughs in the hot time of the year?

Smoky crossed over out of the bleak old log barn.

"Dowelled," he said. "Every dang' rafter in there was dowelled into place by hand . . . not a nail in the whole blessed barn."

Mike eased down on the trough's rough edge, pushed back his hat, and looked around the silent yard. Out of nowhere a robin came winging. She landed in the overhead cottonwood branches and peered critically downward.

"Must live around here," opined Smoky as the bird sang out. "Funny, isn't it, how a feller . . . especially an old feller . . . gets close to things when he lives alone?"

"Yeah."

"Wonder how he worked his cattle? That chute and those working corrals next to the barn show plenty of use. But he was pretty old, wasn't he? Must have been right hard on him, without a cowboy or two on the place."

Mike said—"Yeah."—again. A little twinge of conscience troubled him. He stood up off the trough. "Any hay in the barn?" he asked, strolling over that way.

Smoky stepped out beside him. "Few tons and cut just right, too, with the kernels ripenin' and the joints sweet and green."

The log barn was a massive, lofty structure with bone-dry mud chinking and a raked floor clean enough to eat off. Smoky strongly approved of this and also of how the sets of chain harness had been carefully soaped and properly hung on spaced pegs. In a gloomy corner an ancient saddle of early-day manufacture hung forlornly by one stirrup, a skiff of light dust covering it. Beside this also hung a spade bit with silver-overlaid cheek pieces fixed to a shiny old headstall.

Mike crossed to this dingy place, stood there gloomily eyeing these tools of the stockman's trade, and only looked away when Smoky stepped to the barn door, looked out, stepped back, and said: "Someone's coming. Two fellers on horseback."

Mike listened for the sounds of those oncoming riders without moving. "Neighbors, probably," he said. "Heard we were here more than likely."

Smoky looked out again. For a long while he said nothing more, but gradually his forehead puckered, his heavy brows drew down, and his face curdled into an unpleasant expression.

"If they're neighbors," he eventually growled, "they're the kind we sure don't need many of. Come over here. They're kicking down the rail fence around your uncle's meadow."

Mike walked over and gazed northward. The two strangers were 400 or 500 feet out. Each was holding his horse behind him and each of them was kicking loose the stacked fence liners for a space of about 100 feet in both directions. Those men worked as men do who know exactly why they're doing something. This reason was not difficult to figure out, either. Halfmoon's hay meadow was entirely fenced in by a post-and-rail type old log fence. Those cowboys were deliberately wrecking that fence so that drifting cattle could get in where the lush meadow grass grew.

Mike stepped out of the barn, swung north, and walked 200 feet out, before either of those riders saw him. Smoky was behind him but easily fifty feet on Mike's right. One of the strangers growled something to his companion, then both of them drew upright as they turned toward Ayers.

For a moment no one spoke. Mike saw the Flying E shoulder brand on both those saddled horses. "Who do you work for?" he called ahead.

One of the rough-looking range riders scowled and remained silent. His companion, younger and less reticent, said: "Cy Eagleton's Flying E outfit . . . what's it to you, stranger?"

Mike started forward again without answering this drawled insolence. When he was fifty feet from those two with Smoky farther off to his right, he motioned with his left hand.

"Start putting that fence up again, Flying E."

Neither of those two cowboys moved, but the older one, appraising Ayers's tied-down six-gun in its flesh-out holster, the way Ayers was standing there, and the look on his face, turned uneasy. This one drifted his gaze out to Smoky Buel and back again. He and his companion were caught flat-footed; he knew that. They were close together while their opponents were spread out. If trouble came, they were going to get it good. This one cleared his throat, spat, and said: "Easy, mister. What right you got to tell us to put that fence up again?"

"A fair right," said Ayers dryly. "I own this place. Pete Frazier was my uncle. And while we're on the subject, when my pardner and I rode in we saw an awful lot of Flying E cattle on Halfmoon range. On your way home . . . after you set this fence up again . . . round up as many as you can and take 'em back with you."

"Just like that," snarled the younger cowboy. "Mister, strangers in this country step easy around Flying E. You'd better learn that."

"Shut up," growled the older cowboy to his companion.

The younger man turned to put an indignant look upon the older man. But that one wasn't heeding his partner; he was studying Mike Ayers. "We'll set the fence back up, mister," the older one said, "but as for movin' the cattle off Halfmoon, you'd better talk to Cy Eagleton about that."

Mike lost a little of his stiffness. Smoky, too, out where he stood heard gruff surrender in the older man's tone. He started walking inward.

That was when the younger man made his angry mistake. He thought everyone was off guard and went for his gun, his expression twisting into a look of fierce outrage. The older cowboy was slightly to one side and behind the younger one. He afterward described Mike Ayers's draw as simply a blur and a flash. He swore he didn't see the gun come out at all, didn't even see Mike move until that evil lash of orange flame erupted, and the younger man bumped into him violently from close impact, his face suddenly wire-tight in purest astonishment, his own right hand still upon his holstered gun. Then the younger man fell, rolled once, and flattened with a stillness that had no counterpart in life, shot through the head.

But the older cowboy was fair about it, later, when he told the story. Ayers, he said, had been provoked into it. He hadn't gone for his gun until the dead man had forced him to.

But, although this mitigated what had happened somewhat, along with the fact that both Flying E men were tearing down a fence where they had no right to be actually, there were still enough people around who'd read John Arnold's editorial to remember what it had said about gunfighters not being wanted in Washoe County. These were the ones who added fuel to the fire down in Alturas when Cyrus Eagleton brought in his dead cowboy bumping along gently, head down over his bloody saddle, demanding that Lew Burton go up to Halfmoon and arrest Mike Ayers for murder.

Cy Eagleton was a power in the community. He was a lank, saturnine man of indeterminate years who'd come up out of Texas seven years before to start putting together a cow empire. He wasn't arrogant, but he was aloof and cold toward the townspeople. He made it a point to hire only Texans to ride for him and he made no secret of it that any insult offered his riders was an insult to him, too.

But Eagleton had money, 4,000 head of cattle, and the power that goes with both in a cow country. Alturas' merchants needed him more than he needed them; they made it a practice to look the other way when Flying E riders shot up the town or started brawls in the saloons. They didn't like it. In fact, they didn't like Cyrus Eagleton, but Flying E money ran like a silver stream into their cash drawers, and they liked that very much.

When Eagleton and Lew Burton met in the dust outside Lew's jailhouse and exchanged a long stare over the limp body of Eagleton's dead rider, there was no mistaking the crisis that had come so suddenly to Alturas on that hot, steely midsummer day. What had been avoided for seven years could no longer be avoided. Either Flying E or Alturas must triumph now; there could be no compromise. Both those staring men understood this.

IV

"Well," said Eagleton from the height of his saddle, "are you going after him, or aren't you?"

"I'll go after him," said Burton. "There'll be the usual coroner's inquest, Mister Eagleton. But from what your man said it was a fair fight."

"Yeah? Well, the next one might not be so fair, Sheriff. Who's that feller think he is, anyway?"

"I can't tell you who he thinks he is, Mister Eagleton," said Lew. "But I can tell you his name. It's Mike Ayers."

Eagleton's forehead puckered a little as though he was trying to recollect something. "Ayers?" he said. "Ayers? Wait a minute . . . Mike Ayers, Sheriff, *the* Mike Ayers?"

"Yes."

"No," mumbled Eagleton, really frowning now. "Not that one. Not the gunfighter."

"The same, Mister Eagleton."

Eagleton tossed the lead shank to his dead rider's horse to one of his listening cowboys. "Take him down to the embalming shed," he ordered, never once removing his stare from Lew Burton. "Whatever the cost, tell Doc to bill Flying E." He returned his cold attention to Lew Burton and for a little while just sat there, looking down.

Lew said: "Ayers was Pete Frazier's nephew. I checked on him this morning. He's got legal title by virtue of inheritance, as the courthouse fellers say, to Halfmoon Ranch, lock, stock, and barrel."

"A professional killer, Sheriff. I've heard the stories. Yet you got the guts to say that there was a fair fight."

Lew's temper rose a notch. "Listen, Mister Eagleton, your own man said it was a fair fight. You weren't there, and neither was I, so, until you and I hear different, we'll have to go by that eyewitness' account." Lew stepped back onto the plank walk in front of his office. "All right?" he asked.

"No, it's not all right. I don't give a damn if that killer's Billy the Kid. I want him brought in and tried."

"That," retorted Burton, "is legal procedure and I think you know that it is. So he'll be brought in and he'll be tried."

Eagleton's riders looked at one another. It was obvious that Sheriff Burton was running out of patience. Eagleton, too, sensed this. He clasped one hand over the other atop his saddle horn and gazed hard down at Lew.

"I get the feeling you're not against having men like Ayers in your county, Sheriff. I get the feelin' you'd even like to see this Ayers tangle with me. Well, let me say this, I've met my share of gunfighters before an' I'm still around while they aren't. Put that in your damned pipe and smoke it."

Eagleton spun his horse, jerked his head at the Flying E men, and went clattering northward up Main Street with no regard for the other traffic. Beyond town he slowed to a jolting trot and kept this up for as long as Lew Burton watched.

"I told you," someone growled behind Lew. "Doggone it, Lew, I told you Eagleton'd make trouble."

Burton turned. Ed Grosson was standing there. Elsewhere, spectators were solemnly walking off, some speaking back and forth, others saying nothing, only looking grave and a little apprehensive, as they went along out of the scorching midday sun smash.

"You told me," snapped Lew, swinging to enter his office. "If you're so damned wise, Ed, tell me what comes next."

Grosson stepped in out of the heat, mopped his face, and said: "Sure, bad trouble between Eagleton and Ayers. I'll even guess further than that. Ayers'll get buried and Cy Eagleton will be rougher to get on with than ever."

Lew went around to his desk, dropped down, blew out a gusty breath, and tossed his hat down, hard. "I'll disagree on that. In fact, I'll give you two-to-one odds on Ayers."

"What! Eagleton's got six Flying E Texans, as rough a crew as there is in Nevada. They'll grind Ayers up and spit him out in little pieces."

"Put your money where your mouth is," said Burton. "I'll put a hundred dollars on Ayers, an', if you ever so much as breathe a word of this to anyone, I'll slit your right ear and pull your arm through it."

Grosson put his head skeptically to one side, passed over to a chair, and sat down. "Nope, I won't bet with you," he said. "You know something or you wouldn't be putting up that kind of money."

"The only thing I know for sure, Ed, is that no one eats men like Mike Ayers for breakfast. Not if they're forewarned, and Ayers is now, if he wasn't before."

The banker slumped where he sat, dolorously wagged his head, and mopped sweat. "Trouble," he mumbled. "Dog-gone it, Lew, it's too hot for trouble."

Burton watched Grosson's face a moment, then composed himself. There was more to Grosson's concern than worry over a possible shoot-out in town between Eagleton and Ayers. Lew sat there, waiting.

"Eagleton can't stand a range war, Lew. It's simple economics."

"Yeah," Burton said dryly, and yawned. "Whatever that means."

"He can't afford it. That kind of fighting costs a lot of money. What's sticking in my craw is that he won't think of that. He'll just go ahead and hire some high-priced gunmen, and the bank loan's not set up for expenses like that."

Lew's gaze swiveled around in mild surprise. "Are any bank loans ever set up to finance range wars, Ed?"

Grosson side-stepped that one. He said: "We worked it all out on paper with Eagleton. How much he got for land purchases, how much for purebred polled bulls, how much for water hole development. He's got to stick to our schedules."

"Wait a minute!" exclaimed Sheriff Burton. "Let me get something straight in my mind. Are you saying that you made this loan money available to Eagleton for these specified expenditures, and now you're afraid he'll use the money for his fight with Mike Ayers?"

"In a nutshell that's it, yes."

"Well, hell, just cut off the supply of money."

"Can't. It's already deposited in his account and we got back the recorded chattel mortgages."

Burton digested all this slowly. He was not and

never had been much of a financier. After a while he scratched his head, looked perplexed, and said: "I always thought Cyrus Eagleton was a rich man."

"He is, dog-gone it."

"Then why did he have to borrow bank money, Ed?"

"Listen," explained Grosson impatiently, "there are a lot of rich cowmen who prefer using bank funds and payin' bank interest to using their own money. Don't ask me to explain the thinking behind that kind of reasoning. All I can tell you is that the banks are happy they think that way."

"All right. Then why worry about Eagleton? If he's got money besides what he got from you, he could pay for his range war."

But Grosson shook his head at this. "Who can say how much that kind of a fight will cost, Lew? Who can say how it will end or even who will be alive when it's over? Listen, when a hot-tempered man like Eagleton takes it into his head to fight . . . the sky's the limit. *That's* what's worrying me right now. He could fight himself down to nothing and he'd do it, too. I know Cyrus Eagleton. He's bull-headed an' mean an' proud, which is a bad combination when it comes to fightin' folks."

Lew Burton gazed out the open door. Afternoon shadows were puddling out there. He sighed and pushed upright. "I'll miss supper sure," he said, looking resigned and unhappy. "It'll take me until after dark to get up to Halfmoon, then it'll take me until midnight to fetch Ayers back and lock him up."

The banker also stood up, and, although he had no such bitter prospect staring him in the face as that long ride, he looked just as unhappy as Lew Burton did.

"Listen," he said, "try and talk some sense into Ayers. Try and get him to sell out or lease Halfmoon, or just put the place up for sale and ride on. Ranching's hard work, anyway, and he won't like it. He's not the type."

Lew jerked his head for Grosson to walk outside. After the banker had complied, Lew closed and locked the jailhouse door, nodded wordlessly to Grosson, and started up the plank walk toward the livery barn.

Afternoon shadows were long and getting longer. Over at the blacksmith shop two men were closing the street side doors. At the *Clarion* office Evelyn came out, looked over, saw Sheriff Burton passing into the barn, and stepped down into the roadway dust to strike out after him.

Lew called for his animal, watched the hostler amble indifferently off, removed his hat, and swiped sweat from his forehead with a limp shirt sleeve, crushed the hat back on, and turned as Evelyn spoke his name from the roadside doorway.

"Was it justified?" Evelyn asked without any preamble. "How did it happen, Uncle Lew?"

"Two of Eagleton's boys went over to run some Flying E cattle into Frazier meadow. Ayers caught 'em at it. One got his neck bowed and Ayers killed him. That's as much as I know about it, Evvie. I'm on my way out now to bring Ayers in. We'll have a coroner's hearin' in the morning."

"I saw Eagleton and his riders bring the body in. Dad talked to Lefty Doolin."

"I suppose," said Lew as the hostler came up leading his horse, "John is over there writing another of those editorials of his." He mumbled thanks to the hostler, drew his animal up close, and stepped across to him. As he reined over, Evelyn stepped out to halt beside his animal's shoulder, looking up gravely.

"No," she said. "He wrote it, but I didn't set the type. He won't know until tomorrow when he reads the proofs that I left it out of the paper altogether."

Lew smiled. "Thanks, Evvie, I appreciate that."

"Uncle Lew, tell me something frankly and honestly. What is your private opinion of this Mike Ayers?"

"You've seen him, Evvie. You're a pretty good judge. . . ."

"I've never set eyes on the man in my life."

Lew's eyebrows lifted. "He was in town all day yesterday. Everyone saw him. At least, I thought they had. Whenever I looked out, folks were just happening by the boarding house window, lookin' in. He's got quite a reputation."

"Well, I wasn't one of the curious," Evelyn said tartly. "Now, tell me honestly, Uncle Lew . . . what do you think of him?"

"He's a human being as far as I'm concerned, Evvie. I wasn't put here on earth to judge folks, only to laugh at 'em and sometimes toss 'em in a cell until they sober up."

"Uncle Lew," said Evelyn Arnold, her voice turning a little grim toward the sheriff.

"All right, all right. I think he deserves his chance just like everyone else. He strikes me as being the kind to make a good friend and a good enemy. I'd say he's neither a liar nor a thief, and in this world, honey, when you can say that about a man, you're saying quite a lot."

"You like him?"

"Well, let's just say I'd trust him. Now, Evvie, I've

got a long ride before me and you've got to get along home and fix John's supper." Lew smiled, winked, and eased his horse out into the dusky roadway.

Far out an enormous red disc was hanging suspended in a brassy sky. On both sides of it, soiled cloud streamers were strewn east and west, and below a tired, hot earth was heaving a long sigh after the furious scorch of another midsummer day.

For a long time after Lew Burton rode out of Alturas a vague shade of coppery red covered everything. This was the quiet time, the drowsy period between day's ending and the first cool gloom of evening. If a man had to be astride at all in midsummer Nevada, this was the time to do it, and an old-timer like Alturas' lawman knew this as well as anyone did. What he didn't know, and what he thought about all the way up into the Horseshoe Hills, was what his reception would be at Halfmoon when Ayers and Buel heard what had brought him up there.

V

It was one of the lesser facts of life that worrying over something always made it much larger than it actually was. Lew found that out for the hundredth time when he stepped down in the Halfmoon ranch yard, looped his reins, and hiked up onto the verandah of the main house where orange lamp glow shone. He had his hand fisted and raised in front of the door when a quietly drawling voice hit him from behind.

" 'Evening, Sheriff. You're out kind of late, aren't you?"

Burton turned. Smoky Buel stepped out of shadows, half smiling. He stepped up, grasped the door latch, and pushed. A big square of warm light engulfed Lew and behind the table lamp inside stood Mike Ayers with a shotgun. Those two exchanged looks. Ayers put aside the weapon and said: "We heard the horse long before we decided to be ready, Sheriff. Come on in."

Lew entered, sniffed at the moldiness, looked around at this familiar old room, and crossed to a leather chair, sank down in it, and said nothing until Buel came in, closed the door, and leaned on it.

"Maybe you can guess why I came up here," he said to Mike. "But in case you can't . . . Eagleton came into town today with his whole crew."

Ayers looked wry. "Sure," he said softly. "Would you care for some supper?"

"No thanks."

"Coffee? Smoky just made a fresh pot."

"Well, all right. One cup."

Buel walked away from the front door, disappeared into a back room, and, over the sounds he made, Ayers said: "Was that other one with Eagleton? There were two of 'em. I didn't ask their names. The other one was older. He saw the whole thing. In fact, he tried to talk the younger one out of it."

"Yes, he was with Eagleton. That one's name is Turk Mahoney. He's an old Flying E hand. He told me you were forced into it, but there's still got to be a coroner's inquest. That's the law."

"I know. That's why you're here now, isn't it, to take me back?"

Lew nodded, turning to accept the crockery mug of black java Smoky had brought him. He said nothing until Ayers had his cup, too, then he wagged his head back and forth. "I'm not saying you could have avoided it, Ayers, but I'm sayin' it would've been a heap better for you if it hadn't happened. Folks hereabouts, like I told you before, accept newcomers on trial. This isn't going to smell very good to 'em."

"You think he should've let that punk shoot him?" asked Smoky from his perch upon a little corner stool.

Lew shot Smoky a look but did not reply to this. He said instead: "Your reputation would make folks a little stand-offish by itself. But this killing a man within forty-eight hours after riding in . . . that's going to influence a lot of thinking."

"Especially," said Mike Ayers, balancing his untouched cup of coffee, "with Eagleton and his crew spreading all kinds of wild stories."

"That, too, more'n likely," assented Burton. "But

Turk Mahoney's testimony will scuttle most of that kind of talk, I think. At least it will as far as the trial's concerned."

Ayers drank, set his cup aside, and said: "When is this trial, Sheriff?"

"Tomorrow morning. We'll get it over with just as soon as I can fill out the papers for the judge."

"Jury trial, Sheriff?"

"Naw, this is just a hearing. The judge sits up there taking the evidence. It's a sort of preliminary trial. If you're found justified, you walk out a free man. If you're found guilty, you'll be released on bond and bound over for a regular jury trial."

"You don't sound very grim about it."

"Why should I? Mahoney was the only witness. He told me how it happened, said you had no choice but to shoot. That's all the evidence, except your testimony, that'll be offered. You'll be turned loose."

Lew stood up, finished his coffee, and nodded over at Smoky Buel. "Thanks," he said. "That hit the spot." He turned back to Ayers. "Well, you ready to ride?"

Smoky stood up, too. He was scowling a little, looking more exasperated than anxious. "Now we'll have to put off makin' our tally," he mumbled. "It's always something."

Ayers scooped up his hat, dumped it on the back of his head, and shrugged. "You can tinker around here until I get back, Smoky. We're not in any big hurry anyway."

He and Lew Burton got mounted and left the Halfmoon yard in a slow walk. Behind them, leaning upon a verandah upright, Smoky stood glumly watching their departure down the bland, star-brightened night. After a while he yawned prodigiously, turned, and ambled back inside.

A little bunch of gaunt cattle appeared southward on Halfmoon range walking single-file toward water. At the appearance of two horsemen they lost their lethargy and bolted. Mike watched them go, said— "Flying E."—with a caustic emphasis to that name, and followed this up with a mild curse.

"It's free range country," put in Lew Burton. "You don't want someone's critters on you, it's up to you to push 'em off. It's not up to their owners to come and get 'em."

"I figure to push 'em off, Sheriff, and I understand about free range law. But it's not common for neighbors to deliberately herd their cattle onto another man's grass anywhere I've ever been."

"Do you know Eagleton did that? Did you see his men drive those cattle over here?"

Mike looked around, made a hard little chuckle, and rode along without answering. Of course he hadn't seen the Flying E push its cattle onto Halfmoon range, but both he and Sheriff Burton knew that was what had happened.

A few miles farther down out of the Horseshoe Hills, Ayers said musingly: "Tell me about this Cyrus Eagleton, Sheriff. It's beginning to look like I've got a worthwhile enemy there. What kind of a man is he?"

"Long, lean Texan. Came to Washoe County about seven years back. Doesn't mix much with local folks. Hires only Texas hands. Has made money and built up quite a sizable spread. That's about the size of it where Eagleton's concerned. He and his Texas boys are pretty clanny. If one of them gets into trouble, all the others come a-running."

"You don't sound as though you like him."

"I don't dislike him. Up to now he's paid the fines when his boys get wild and bust things up in town. There are times when he's kind of cantankerous, but folks in Alturas mostly overlook that. He spends a lot of money among the stores in town, pays up prompt, and knows what he wants."

"What did my uncle think of him?"

Lew's brow wrinkled. He had no trouble recalling some of the quietly pithy things old Pete had said to him about Cy Eagleton, but he didn't think repeating them now would help anyone, so all he said was: "They got along."

Mike looked amused at this but he probed no deeper. He didn't think he had to. He'd made his appraisal of Lew Burton and had come up with a very close and correct assessment of the lawman. Lew was one of those quiet men who tried harder to settle disputes than he did to force them to showdowns. He was tolerant of the shortcomings of others and had spent more than half a lifetime trying to get others to be likewise. The trouble with that philosophy, Mike thought privately, was that it overlooked the raw edges human nature was inherently endowed with. He didn't like trouble, either, but he'd long ago come to a tough realization that not very many troublesome people could be placated— especially Texans. That kind only understood one thing—force.

They were in sight of Alturas before either of them spoke again. Little yonder pinpricks of lamplight lay low upon the faint-lighted plain and far back stood those barren hillsides where the Horseshoe Hills formed a kind of uninviting bastion.

Ayers said: "I had an idea, when I came down

here, that maybe things might be a little different for me from here on. When a man gets close to thirty, Sheriff, he isn't content with the wild life any more. He slows down a little in his thinking, gets to miss some of the things other men have. But I could be wrong about that settling down business."

Lew remembered what Ed Grosson had said to him and repeated it now. "You could sell out. Eagleton wouldn't haggle over the price of Halfmoon. Ranching's hard work and there'd be plenty of other places a feller could start afresh without any handicap like you're facing here."

But Ayers didn't accept this. "Something I learned long ago is that when a man moves from unpleasantness, he doesn't ever really leave it behind. Sure, I could sell to this Eagleton feller, but there are two things wrong with that, an' both of 'em rub me the wrong way. One is that I'd be lettin' him think he'd run me out. The other is that I've got a feeling my uncle'd turn over in his grave."

"That last part's right enough," retorted Lew. "I think you've about got it figured out by now that old Pete didn't have much use for Cy Eagleton." Lew changed course slightly so as to strike the north entrance into town. "As for the other part, my boy, every man's got to live with himself."

They passed quietly down the dark roadway pacing in and out of alternating squares of lamplight from the variety houses, gambling halls, and saloons, until, in front of the jailhouse, they both drew rein and got stiffly down. "I'll care for the horses later," said Lew. "Come on inside and I'll return your favor with a cup of java. By the way, if you're hungry, I can fetch you something from the café. It's a long time till morning."

Mike accepted the offer of coffee but declined the food. There was something about the prospect of being jailed that destroyed a man's appetite. He entered Burton's office, waited until Lew lit a lamp, drew his six-gun, and put it upon the lawman's desk while Lew busied himself over the little cook stove.

"Something's been in the back of my mind for the last couple of hours, Sheriff," he said. "This judge who'll hear the evidence tomorrow, is he one of the folks who'll likely be prejudiced against me?"

Lew set the pot over the flame hole, consulted his watch meticulously, put the watch away, and said: "Naw, Judge Harper's been on the bench thirty years. His own wife couldn't influence him in favor of his own son. I don't see that you've got a thing to worry about."

Lew crossed over, saw Ayers's gun lying there, and nodded at this. He gestured for the prisoner to have a seat, sat down himself, and began writing something on a printed form. Twice he halted at this to consult his watch and, the last time he got up, crossed over to the stove and poured two cups of coffee.

"Exactly seven minutes," he said. "Any longer and it gets stout enough to float a horseshoe."

Ayers grinned; it was hard not to like this burly, graying man with his amusing idiosyncrasies and his quiet manner. "I'll have to tell Smoky that. He's the salt of the earth, but, by golly, he makes the lousiest coffee I ever tasted."

Lew looked up from his writing to make a rueful small smile. "I noticed that," he agreed. "I noticed that right off. Now, I got to take a statement from you on just how that fight took place. Talk slow because I'm not a very good transcriber."

Ayers sipped coffee, recounted everything he re-membered of the killing of that Flying E cowboy, and, when he finished, he said: "One question, Sher-iff. Will that dog-gone newspaperman who raked me over the coals in that editorial get a copy of this?"

"He can get the court transcript when the hear-ing's over. There's no law against him doing that. And if I know John Arnold, he'll get it and write another editorial. But let me tell you something about John. He says it's his duty to give all the news, but he's fair."

Ayers raised his eyebrows at this last statement.

"Yeah," said Lew, pushing on, "I know what you're thinking. But you're wrong. He won't rake you un-less he's convinced you deserve it. Regardless of what some folks believe, John tries to be factual and fair. Sometimes that's darn' near got him worked over, but I'd rather try to change the spots on a leop-ard than change John's idea of his duty." Lew con-sidered his completed form skeptically, erased two words, substituted others in their places, and tossed down his pencil. "One more thing about John Ar-nold. If you'd tangled with anyone but Cyrus Ea-gleton, he might've been a little rougher on you."

"I see. He doesn't like Eagleton, either."

Lew tilted his chair back, rubbed his eyes, and took up the coffee cup before replying to this. "He doesn't like Flying E's high-handed way of operat-ing. John's one of those scribes who's always cham-pioning the common man. When there's no common man involved, he invents one. He's said half a dozen times in his editorials that Cyrus Eagleton has no regard for the common man of Washoe County." Lew drained his cup, smacked his lips, and wryly smiled. "Tell me something, Mister Ayers, just who the hell is the common man anyway? I've lived near fifty years and I'll be hanged if I ever met him."

Those two exchanged a chuckle over this, then Lew took Ayers to a strap-steel cage in his back room and locked Ayers in for the night. The last thing he said to his prisoner was: "I wouldn't worry about the trial if I were you. Turk Mahoney's testimony'll have you back at Halfmoon before suppertime."

And that was perhaps the most incorrect prediction Lew Burton had ever made in his long lifetime.

VI

The trial of Mike Ayers was held upstairs over the Alturas Volunteer Fire Brigade's storehouse. It was held in a garret-like room with what Mike thought was more than enough space, but he was wrong there because, before the elderly, craggy-faced old judge appeared, every bench in that low-ceilinged room was jammed with people. Spectators were about equally divided between range men and townsmen. There were several dozen women, mostly from the dance halls and saloons, but women nevertheless.

There were no attorneys. The judge took his seat, rapped for order, leaned upon his table, and skewered Sheriff Burton with a pair of eyes resembling ice chips. "The evidence," he said in a gravelly tone, and never once looked at either Mike Ayers or Cy Eagleton, the latter seated on a front-row bench flanked by his rough crew of Texans.

Lew picked up a paper, read off it giving the bare essential facts, gazed over at the judge as though awaiting questions, and, when none came, Lew sat back down.

Now the judge looked down at Mike Ayers. He said not a word for the space of thirty seconds. It was as though he were plumbing the very soul of the prisoner. Finally he flicked a leathery hand.

"Your version," he said dispassionately, and all the time Ayers was speaking, old Harper never once looked away from him. When Mike finished, the judge gave him an infinitesimal nod.

"Sit down," he ordered, and Mike sat.

Cyrus Eagleton straightened on his bench. His riders, too, perked up. The judge said: "Anyone else?" And Eagleton threw out a hand toward the dark, older cowboy among his men whose name was Turk Mahoney. The judge nodded as though he had known in advance about Mahoney.

"Stand up, give your name and your statement," he grumbled, propped his head in both hands, and stared down in that flinty way he had.

Mahoney identified himself, cleared his throat, shot a quick look at Mike Ayers, and licked his lips. The judge and everyone else waited. Cyrus Eagleton's black brows dropped a little with impatience. Mahoney saw this, cleared his throat again, and said: "Me 'n' the dead man rode into Halfmoon's yard headin' for the house. It was late afternoon, near evening. That Ayers feller an' his pardner come out and challenged us. We tried to explain what we was there for . . . lookin' for stray Flyin' E cattle. That Ayers feller over there . . . he cursed at us, went for his gun, an', before I could cry out we was there peaceable, he'd dropped my pardner from less'n fifty feet with a slug through his brain."

Lew Burton was sitting there with his jaw hanging slack, staring up at Mahoney. Mike Ayers, his face a blank mask, very slowly swung his gaze from Mahoney to Eagleton. These two exchanged a look. Eagleton's lips lifted a little at their outer corners in a very faint, vicious little smile, then dropped, turning his face expressionless except for the satisfied, bleak look in his sunken, set eyes.

For a while the silence in the room was almost a physical thing, then Judge Harper dropped his arms, leaned back, and looked from Mahoney to Ayers and on over to Lew Burton.

"Where's this prisoner's pardner?" he asked. "He was there, I gather. Why didn't you fetch him in, too, Sheriff?"

Lew slowly closed his mouth. He met the judge's stony gaze with rusty color mounting up from his throat all the way to his hairline. "I didn't figure it'd be necessary," he said huskily.

"Not necessary?" said the judge acidly. "We have two separate versions of this killing. One or the other of these men is lying. One or the other of them needs supporting evidence. Did you think to deny the prisoner corroborating substantiation, Sheriff?"

Lew's face was brick red. He shook his head, riffled through the papers before him, looked at Mike, at Turk Mahoney, then back to the judge. "No, sir," he said in a low, roughened tone of voice. "Mahoney told an entirely different story yesterday. He said Ayers was forced to draw and that it was in his opinion a fair. . . ."

"Sheriff! Hearsay evidence's no damn' good and you know it. I don't want to hear any more." Harper took up his little gavel, held it suspended, and glared down at Lew. "I'm surprised at you, man. Now you get Ayers's pardner in here and let's have this trial held in true legal fashion." The gavel descended, hard, Judge Harper stood up to his full bony height, and he scowled out over the room. "This trial is postponed until the same time tomorrow. The prisoner is remanded into custody. Court dismissed . . . Sheriff Burton, please remain."

Mike, seated beside Burton, quietly sighed. He heard Eagleton and his men stamping around behind him, but he did not look back; he was studying that bony old tough-faced judge up there behind his table. He thought Lew Burton's assessment of Clarence Harper was about correct, that old attorney wouldn't be swayed by anything but the facts, the evidence presented before him, and the legal codes that governed both.

Lew turned to say something, but at that precise moment old Harper flicked his coat tails, re-seated himself, snorted, and said: "Lew, what the hell's wrong with you? You getting old or something? You almost got Mister Ayers set squarely upon a scaffold platform."

Burton looked around, saw that the room was empty except for the three of them and a bored, balding man who was the clerk and who was ignoring everything except the cigar he was lighting, and said: "Clarence, this thing was pure routine. Mahoney said Ayers killed that cowboy after being forced into it. I give you my word that's exactly what he told me yesterday in my office. Hell, I had no idea he'd do an about-face like this."

"Well, Lew, you should've expected something, you know." The judge gathered up his papers, frowned at them, carefully aligned the corners, and raised his bleak eyes once more. "I can't gaze into a crystal ball for the facts. You've got to give them to me. You and Ayers and Mahoney." The judge put up a thin hand, pinched the bridge of his nose, dropped the hand, and got up again, this time with an unmistakable air of finality. "Lock your prisoner up again, Lew, subpoena his sidekick, get 'em both in here to testify tomorrow morning, and let's not have any more slip-ups. Dammit, I've got to be over at Vegas for a trial day after tomorrow and this postponement's likely to spoil my schedule."

The judge turned and walked angrily down from his little raised platform, hiked right past Lew and Mike Ayers without another word or glance at either, and trooped on out of the courtroom. He slammed the door as he departed, slammed it hard.

Lew picked up his hat, dumped it on his head, and carefully folded the papers he'd brought with him, put them into a pocket, and not until he'd completed all this did he turn to face Mike Ayers. He was very uncomfortable.

"I guess we go back to jail," he said, having a little trouble facing Mike's calm eyes. "I guess I don't have any real excuse to give you, either. Judge Harper's right . . . I should've expected something like that. Only, by golly, it just never occurred to me, not after the forthright way Mahoney told his story yesterday."

Ayers stood up, nodded his head, turned and started toward the door. He didn't speak and this made Lew feel even more guilty and uncomfortable.

Back out in the summer-glazed roadway people stood in little groups along the sidewalks, talking. When Ayers and Burton emerged, most of this talk dwindled. Mike walked quietly along and was halfway across the dusty, heat-faded roadway, when behind him a man's mirthless low laugh rang out. Ayers turned, looking for the man who'd made that sound, found him, and fixed this man with his steady gaze.

Lew looked back, too. He brushed Ayers's arm saying: "Never mind. That's Lefty Doolin, Eagleton's foreman. He's a bully and worse. Come along."

Mike fixed Doolin's fiery red face in his mind. Doolin didn't laugh again; he simply stood back there with several other lounging, hard-eyed Flying E cowboys, both thumbs hooked in his shell belt, sardonically smiling at Mike Ayers. He was a red-headed, red-faced, hard, and capable-looking man of stocky build whose sloping shoulders and knife-slash mouth indicated power and ruthlessness.

Something fierce passed between these two as they exchanged that wintry stare, then Doolin softly said: "You'll learn, gunfighter. You'll learn . . . if you live long enough."

Lew swung, his lips flattened and his squinted eyes flashing fire points. "One more word, Lefty, and I'll put you in the same cell with him."

Doolin's lips parted as though to speak, but in the end Eagleton's range boss said nothing. He simply stood there, knee-sprung, thumbs hooked, his red face creased into that knowing, unfriendly smile.

Mike turned and continued on to the jailhouse with Lew Burton. Inside again, where the mid-morning heat had not yet reached, he stopped, considered his six-gun where it still lay on Burton's desk, and spoke for the first time since leaving the courtroom.

"I think, Sheriff, your friend Eagleton's a lot tougher than you figured him to be. I got the impression in that courtroom that he's not out to frame me just for that shoot-out. He's out for a lot more. You reckon it could be Halfmoon?"

Lew caught the sarcasm in Ayers's tone and didn't answer that question. He said instead: "I don't blame you for bein' mad. I pulled a real boner this morning."

"Forget that part of it," said Ayers. "I've been

overnight in jailhouses before. What's bothering me now is just how far Eagleton's prepared to go. I might have to import a cussed lawyer before I'm safe from a hanging."

Lew dropped down at his desk, picked up Ayers's six-gun, opened a drawer, and dropped it in, closed the drawer, and shook his head. "I've got to ride back up to Halfmoon again, dammit!" he exclaimed. "In the middle part of the day, too." He got up, scooped up his cell-block keys, and started for the back room. "Come on. I've made it a practice for twenty years not to get too involved in my arrest cases, but I'll be damned if I like being made a fool of. Eagleton sure made me look old and silly this morning, so I'll go up and fetch back Buel . . . then, by gawd, we'll see who looks silly tomorrow."

Mike passed along as far as his strap-steel cage and waited while Lew opened the door, admitted him, and locked the door after him, then he said dryly: "I reckon Eagleton's cattle'll get into my meadow, after all. With Smoky down here, too, Mahoney'll kick down the fence again." He looked out at Sheriff Burton speculatively. "I reckon the only way to get to know how folks operate in Washoe County is to rub shoulders with 'em, isn't it?"

"They aren't all like Eagleton, Doolin, and that danged lying Turk Mahoney. Take my word for that."

Ayers stood there, looking as though this did not particularly interest him right now. His expression was gravely thoughtful and, Lew Burton thought, resignedly deadly, as though, in fact, Mike Ayers had been balancing a hard decision in his thoughts and had come at long last to a conclusion that promised no surrender or no peace for the men who had calmly lied him into a spot where his life was actually endangered.

Lew couldn't actually blame Mike Ayers for this, but when he returned to his outer office, threw down the cell keys, and paused a moment at his desk before going along to the livery barn for his horse, he made a promise to himself. The next time he met Turk Mahoney face to face he was going to give Turk a tongue-lashing he'd be unlikely to forget for a long time.

There were two things in this world Lew Burton detested above all others: liars and thieves. He had it in his mind that a man who would be one would also be the other. He left the office, locked the door, and strode toward the livery barn thinking that, after all the years he'd been around Turk Mahoney, he'd never considered him a liar before. It hurt a man's opinion of himself to find he'd been so wrong for so long. Lew's mood was rough when he swung in, called for his horse, and met Amos Darren just returning from somewhere in his red-wheeled buggy.

Amos was sweating, his cheeks were red from summertime exertion, and he gazed a little cynically over at Lew as though the combination of heat and irascibility had somehow made them strangers.

"What'd you do this morning, Sheriff?" Amos asked. "I met some cowmen returning home who'd been at the trial this morning. They told me Clarence Harper took a bite out of your hide for nearly getting that gunfighter hanged by an oversight."

The hostler came up with Lew's saddled animal. He shot a sly look from the sheriff to the saloon man, faded back a little distance, and strained to hear what passed between these two.

"I wish you'd make up your mind," said Lew testily as he mounted. "First, you and Ed Grosson and half the others here in town are for ridin' Ayers out of town on a rail. Now all of a sudden you're on his side against Flying E."

Darren shook sweat off his soft chin. "If a man's got to make a choice like that," he said, "then I guess some of us would side with the gunfighter."

Lew looked down, saying tartly: "Like hell you would. As long as Flying E money buys you things like that red-wheeled runabout, you only dislike Eagleton from a distance. You'd toss Ayers to the wolves in a second, Amos, if you thought you'd lose business by siding with him."

Lew rode out into the bitter yellow sun smash of high noon, set his course for the Horseshoe Hills, and went grumpily along, disgusted with himself, his town, and his townsmen.

VII

It was a poor day for riding. That lemon-yellow sun hung suspended above Washoe County, diluting shadows to gunmetal gray and causing alkali dust to rise up at every small disturbance.

Lew rode along as a Mexican would ride, slump-shouldered, relaxed, and languid. It was the only way to ride in heat like that. He got to the Horseshoe Hills, made a detour in order to put a high hill between himself and that sun, let his animal pick the gait, and came down into Halfmoon's yard a little shy of five o'clock. Dusk would not arrive for another three hours and not for an hour after that would night arrive.

There were some calving heifers in a pole corral, evidence that Smoky Buel hadn't wasted the entire day, but no one came forward to greet Lew. He watered his animal at the trough, led him to a tie stall inside the barn, loosened the saddle, and forked him some timothy hay. Still no one showed up.

He walked out back, thinking it likely that, if Smoky wasn't at the house, he might be at the chutes. But except for those corralled heifers, there was no movement, no other sign of life near the working corrals at all. He did notice two saddle horses in a corral with sweat stains upon their backs as he started to flank the barn on his way to the house. In fact, he walked 100 feet onward before it struck him that he knew one of those horses. He turned, squinted rearward, then slowly turned and slowly hiked back for another look.

Sure enough, that second saddle-stained animal belonged to John Arnold. He asked himself just what the devil old John was doing up here, and in spite of himself Lew felt annoyed by the probable answer. *Danged old fool, him and his duty.* Lew swung around and started for the house again. Why hadn't John come to him instead of riding all the way up here to get his story about the killing of that Flying E rider?

He was within fifty feet of the ranch house front door when someone on ahead cocked a gun. Lew heard that sound and almost simultaneously threw himself sideways, jumping for the thin shelter of a verandah upright and going for his hip-holstered six-gun. He had no time for thought; his actions were instinctive and primitive, the urges of a frontiersman whose instincts for preservation were just below his civilized veneer.

Whoever had cocked that weapon, though, did not fire it. Lew waited, trying to place the location of that sharp, solitary sound, his own gun up and ready. Then a voice spoke out from somewhere inside the house, and Lew's wire-tightness gradually softened, turned slowly, inexorably to hard anger, for that voice belonged to John Arnold.

"Lew," it called, "what're you trying to do . . . get shot?"

Burton holstered his weapon, let off a fierce swear word, and said: "You simpleton, John. Anyone with a lick o' sense looks first . . . then cocks their gun."

"I did look, and you looked like you might've been one of 'em, too."

"One of who? What are you talking about?"

Arnold didn't answer back. He opened the house door, stepped forth with a Winchester in his hand, peered all around, then came mincing toward the place where Lew was watching him.

"One of those men who shot Buel," he said.

Lew's anger dissolved in a twinkling. He stepped away from the post, joined Arnold on the verandah, and halted. The newsman turned without another word and reëntered the house, passed through several rooms with Lew Burton at his heels, paused outside a closed door to lean the carbine there, and entered with Lew almost on his heels.

From an age-blackened old walnut bedstead Smoky Buel was watching the door. At sight of Arnold and Sheriff Burton his face slackened, he sluggishly drew a hand from beneath a blanket, and eased off the hammer of the cocked six-gun in that hand.

"It was the sheriff," said John Arnold to the bedridden man.

Lew crossed to Buel's bedside in two big strides. He examined the scarlet bandage low on Buel's side, looked into the pain-dulled eyes, kicked up a chair, and dropped down upon it.

"Who did it?" he asked.

Buel shook his head weakly. "Damned if I know. I was walkin' from the barn to the house . . . didn't hear a thing, Sheriff, no riders comin', no nothin', then all of a sudden . . . *wham!* . . . I thought the doggone sky'd fallen on me. I reckon whoever drygulched me thought he'd scored good, because there was only that one shot."

"It downed you?"

"Downed me, Sheriff? Hell, it knocked me senseless. When I come to, there was that newspaperman leanin' over me. I. . . ."

"He tried to shoot me," interrupted Arnold. "I'd ridden up to get his version of the Flying E shooting, Lew."

Lew turned toward Arnold. "Did you hear the shot?"

"Yes, but I didn't pay any attention. You know . . . it could've been a pot hunter."

"Did you see anyone ridin' away from Halfmoon?"

Arnold shook his head. "Not a soul. I rode on into the yard, saw Buel lying there all bloody, ran over to see if I could do anything, and he tried to draw his gun on me. I took away his gun, dragged him in here, got him onto the bed, and cleaned up the wound, bandaged it . . . then I heard you out there, thought it might be the assassin coming back and. . . ."

"Yeah," growled Lew, easing back in the chair. "I know the rest." He took off his hat, tossed it aside, looking long at Smoky Buel, then let off a big sigh and bent forward to examine the wound with probing fingers. Twice Buel winced from that experienced hand. Lew straightened up, looked around at John, and said: "How about wrestling us up a pot of coffee before we head down out of these lousy hills with him, John? He's got to see the sawbones down in town. He's got at least two busted ribs."

"Sure," said Arnold, nodding downward at the sticky, clumsy bandages around Buel's middle, "I got the bleedin' pretty well stopped, Lew, but you know more about these things than I do. Maybe you'd better have a look."

Lew nodded; that had been his intention anyway.

After Arnold had left the room, he began re-dressing Buel's injury. For a while neither of them spoke. The wound was a ragged gouge that had cut through skin and deeply into Buel's muscles, but it was a clean injury. Lew had seen other wounds like it. As he worked, he said: "I guess John told you Ayers was bound over for trial tomorrow."

"He told me. He and I figured out something else, too, Sheriff."

"Yeah?" Lew thought he knew what was coming and he was correct.

"Yeah. The court wants my testimony as a witness. Somebody else doesn't want me testifying. That somebody rode up here, waited me out, an', when I got into his sights, he let me have it."

Lew went right on working over the fresh bandaging. He put goose grease next to the hide so the cloth wouldn't stick, and he made a professional padding to absorb blood if bleeding started again. He was also busy in another way; he was thinking that the shooting just about had to have happened the way Buel and John Arnold thought. But where he veered off from those two was in what came next. He didn't want a range war in his county. He didn't want a gunfighter of Mike Ayers's capacity riding any vengeance trail, either. As for Cy Eagleton—he'd have a talk with him, but this time Eagleton wasn't going to have the initiative, big rich cowman or not.

And finally, there was his jailhouse. Men as big as Cyrus Eagleton had been locked in it before. And men as wrathy as Mike Ayers would be when he heard what had happened to his partner had been held there, too.

Lew finished with the bandaging. He wiped his hand and saw Buel's hard gaze upon him. He shrugged. "Maybe and maybe not," he said. "You didn't see the feller who downed you. Before you run off half-cocked, let me explain something to you, Smoky. In murder or attempted murder it takes one of two things to get a conviction. A confession or a witness. You have neither."

"I don't need neither," said Buel. "All I need is a couple of weeks to get over this wound, then I'll work out my own conviction."

John came in with three mugs of black coffee. Nothing more was said for a while. Not until the newspaperman began theorizing about the shooting. Then Sheriff Burton put an ironic stare on Arnold and said: "You write up a bunch of bunk like that you're spouting right now, and Cy Eagleton'll skin you alive an' nail your hide to a wall. You don't know any more who shot Buel than he does or than I do."

Arnold's eyes flashed. "Who else had reason, tell me that, Lew?"

"Listen, John, Mike Ayers has enemies. He's a gunfighter, an' gunfighters got enemies. These two been in Alturas less than a week. Sure it could've been Eagleton. But it's just as likely it was someone you or me don't know a blessed thing about, too. So do us all a favor and don't go hinting in one of your editorials it was Eagleton."

Arnold drank his coffee, watched the sheriff, said no more, but showed by his expression he was a long way from accepting the impossibility that Buel's assassin had not come from Flying E.

Lew put aside his empty cup, stood up, and squinted into the lowering indoor shadows. "I'll go hitch a team to the ranch wagon," he said. "John, round up a mess of blankets and stuff to put Buel on." He looked down, saw how Buel was watching him from feverish and vengeful eyes, crossed to the door, and dourly passed on out of the house.

This, he told himself as he headed for the barn, was just exactly what he didn't need, and he hadn't said that to John Arnold about the possibility of the assassin being someone no one knew because he believed it. He'd said it to gain a little time, to stall Arnold for a few days.

He believed Eagleton was behind the attempted murder of Smoky Buel as firmly as he'd ever believed anything, but there was one facet of law enforcement folks seldom knew anything about, and that was how the meddling of outsiders habitually snarled trails which otherwise were not ordinarily too complicated, particularly when a crime such as this one was sprang directly from the passionate dislike of one man for other men.

There was a hanging lantern in the barn but Lew didn't light it. He harnessed a team to Pete Frazier's old wagon, tossed in a couple of forks full of hay, climbed up, kicked off the brake, and drove out into the yard and across to the house. Evening was rapidly descending now. For a time, although the sun was gone, it would actually get hotter, but by the time they got down out of the hills there would be coolness.

He stepped down in front of the house, noticed that John had lighted a lamp inside, strode through the ajar door, and passed along into the wounded man's room. There, without a word passing between them, he and Arnold lifted husky Smoky Buel, staggered outside with him, and strained upward to deposit him with rough gentleness upon the hay. It took a little time to make him comfortable, to cover him, and throw in some additional clean rags in case they might have to re-bandage him along the way. It was fully dark by the time Arnold went after his horse and Lew leaned over the sideboards gazing down at the injured man.

Buel looked up with a pained face to say: "Sheriff, you don't believe what you told Arnold about maybe it was someone huntin' me 'n' Mike."

"Don't I?"

"Naw. But that's all right with me. I can guess why you said that, an' maybe you're right. At least you ought to know your own county. Arnold was just tellin' me how long you been enforcin' the law here-abouts."

"Care for a smoke?" asked Lew.

"No, thanks."

"If there's any whiskey in the house maybe we'd better fetch it along."

Lew was turning away as though to go back inside when Buel said: "Wait a minute. Let the liquor go. Something I want to tell you."

Lew came back around and leaned there, looking down. "Save it," he said. "It's a long, bumpy haul down to town. You'll need all the strength you've got before we get there."

Buel ignored this. "Sheriff, every damned place I've ever been in has its Cyrus Eagletons. You know the type as well as I do. Well, I'm not tellin' you this to try an' make out that Mike Ayers is any better'n he really is, but it's been the Eagletons who've given him his reputation . . . and his notches. Mike's a fair man. He's no professional killer. He's hired out his gun, sure, but only because it sticks in his craw when these range-hog types get to ridin' rough-shod over folks."

"All right," said Lew quietly. "I'll accept that. I've had a little experience at judgin' men, too, Smoky."

"Let me finish," said Buel. "Eagleton's not through. Downin' me wasn't the big thing for him. Gettin' control of Halfmoon isn't, either. You know what is, Sheriff?"

"I know, Smoky, having someone face him down. Having someone stand up to him."

"Yeah. That's it. Now there's one more thing. Eagleton's rich. He'll hire gun hands, more'n likely. Well, Sheriff . . . Mike don't have to hire 'em. He's got friends from Montana to Texas. All he's got to do is send a few telegrams and your town'll have fifty, a hundred damned good gun hands here within ten days to ride with Mike Ayers."

Lew squinted out where a horseman showed. He stepped away from Buel, swung up onto the wagon seat, took up the lines, and flicked them, easing the wagon out behind John Arnold.

VIII

The ride down out of the Horseshoe Hills was not as bad for Smoky Buel as Lew had thought it would be, but as he knew, the worst a man expects sometimes never comes to pass. They stopped once out upon the star-lighted prairie to give Buel a long pull of spring water from John Arnold's canteen, but that was the only halt they made.

Lew rode up there on the wagon seat, thinking some unpleasant thoughts. He'd never openly opposed Cyrus Eagleton in anything; in fact, he'd made a particular point of stepping lightly around him. Not because he feared Flying E, but rather because as an elected official he had to get along with the merchants and the others in his bailiwick who derived their income from the big cow outfits.

Well, it seemed that what up to now had been avoidable had now become unavoidable—a showdown with Eagleton and his tough Texas crew. There was nothing about this conclusion to make Lew's seamed, sun-darkened features pleasant. Twice John Arnold, riding beside the near front wheel, bent to say something, and twice John caught reflected star shine off Lew's bitter face and straightened back to ride along without speaking.

They came down through the balmy night into Alturas with the watery moon beyond its meridian. Mostly the town was abed, but even the few people who saw them pass down Main Street—Burton's saddle animal tethered to the tailgate, John Arnold outriding beside the team—paid no great attention because it was too dark to see the limp, gray-faced, wounded man down in the wagon bed.

When Lew drew up at the jailhouse, John finally spoke. "Not in there," he said. "That's no place for a sick man, Lew. Follow me over to my place."

Burton looked over, wrinkled his forehead at Arnold, and said: "The jail's clean and besides you don't want to get mixed up in this."

"I'm already mixed up in it," retorted Arnold, reining away. "Come along. I've got plenty of empty bedrooms and Evelyn's a sight better nurse'n you'll be."

Lew clucked at the team. He was too tired to argue; besides, John was right, Evvie could care for Buel better than anyone else.

They swung wide at the first intersecting byway that ran easterly from Main Street, went halfway down this unlighted residential street, and drew in again where a white house was set back behind a picket fence with two lights burning inside.

John went around the back to put up his horse. Lew got down, eased down the tailgate, and looked in at Buel. "Wasn't too bad, was it?" he asked.

Smoky made a weak grin. There was shiny sweat on his upper lip and forehead. "Depends on what you compare it with," he said. "Being dragged behind wild horses or not bein' all shot to hell."

Lew smiled. Across the wagon bed up at the house a door opened. He saw Evelyn step forth and a moment later her father also came out. Those two spoke swiftly back and forth, Evelyn hastened back into the house, and John came down to the front gate.

"How is he?" John asked as he approached the wagon.

"Ready to rush out and cull wildcats," said Lew with a droll wink at Buel.

They got him supported upon their interlocking arms, passed through the gate, up to the house, and inside. Evelyn was there as tense as a wound spring to show them which bedroom to put Buel in. She shot Lew a questioning look that he chose to interpret as referring to the local doctor, and he said: "As soon as I've put up the horses, I'll hunt up Doc and send him around, Evvie."

They got Buel onto a bed and for a while he lay there unmoving, both eyes pinched closed, his mouth sucked back in a contortion of pain, his breathing shallow and bubbly.

John went back out into the night with Lew. As the lawman was unfurling the lines preparatory to climbing back upon the wagon's high seat, he said: "Evvie did something she's never done before, Lew. She cut out my editorial in tomorrow's paper. You put her up to that, didn't you?"

"Not directly, John, but if you're lookin' for someone to blame, go right ahead and lay it on my back, I've got broad shoulders an' I'm used to bein' blamed for things. Only for now, let's not argue about that. I'm dog-tired an' Buel needs the sawbones."

"I wasn't going to argue, Lew. I was going to say . . . she did right."

Lew evened up the lines, looked back to see that his horse was still behind the wagon, looked down, and said: "I never tried to tell you how to run your business in my life, John, but I'd like to make a suggestion to you tonight. Just stand back and see how things go for a day or two before you jump into the middle of this one. All right?"

"All right. Good night, Lew. You've got one more job to do tonight I don't envy you for."

Lew nodded. Arnold meant telling Mike Ayers his partner had been ambushed and nearly killed. He flicked the lines and drove off. He'd had worse chores in his lifetime; even this one could've been worse; it could've turned out that Buel had been killed.

He turned the horses over to the night hawk at the livery barn, walked down to his office, and unlocked the door, sniffed at the mustiness, lit a lamp, and scooped up his cell-block keys, passed through as far as Ayers's cell, and found his prisoner deeply asleep upon a wall bunk. He rattled the door in opening it, entered, waited for Ayers to sit up, yawn, and blink over at him, then he let the gunfighter have it straight from the shoulder.

"I just came back to town from Halfmoon with Smoky Buel in your uncle's old spring wagon, shot in the middle. He's not dead by a long sight, but it was a close thing. I told the liveryman to get the sawbones over to John Arnold's place right away to look at him."

Ayers's yawn froze, his eyes lost all their sleep haziness, and his body stopped moving on the bunk. Lew, leaning upon the front wall of Ayers's cell, stood stoically awaiting the deluge of questions. When they ultimately came, he answered as best he could, walked back out of the cell again, locked the door, and said: "If you're still not hungry, I'll head for bed and see you in the morning."

Ayers rose up, crossed to the door, and looked steadily out. "Never mind the supper," he said.

"Why did you take him to that newspaperman's house?"

"His daughter's exactly what Buel needs right now . . . a good nurse."

"Has it occurred to you," said Ayers thinly, "that Arnold was the only one around when Smoky was shot?"

Lew blinked. "Arnold? John Arnold? You don't know what you're talkin' about. John was up there to get your pardner's version of the shooting. Naw, you're wrong as you can be, Ayers. I've known John Arnold for most of my adult life. I'll bet you he doesn't even own a six-gun, and I know for a fact he never carries one."

"He's got no liking for me, Sheriff, and that would include my sidekick."

"Listen," protested Lew, "you're a stranger here. Sure, I know how you feel right now, but you're dead wrong about John. He's like old Judge Harper, he'd never in this world do anything off-color."

"Then who did?" Ayers demanded. "Eagleton?"

"Maybe," assented Lew grudgingly. "Listen, go on back to bed. I'll see you in the morning. Meanwhile, don't worry, I'll make sure the doctor gets over to see Smoky and I'll see you again first thing in the morning."

Mike Ayers, standing there in the cell-block's eternal windowless gloom, seemed gradually to come down to a kind of wintry acceptance of something. Lew could see this alteration in the gunfighter as he hesitated about leaving. It was a little like watching a drunkard's solid resolution dwindle before the spectacle of a full whiskey bottle, only here, Lew knew, it had nothing to do with drinking.

"All right," the gunfighter said in a normal tone.

"Eagleton wants a war." Ayers didn't finish it. He turned abruptly, crossed back to his bunk, and eased down there, ignoring Lew Burton completely.

For a little longer the sheriff stood there. Tiredness could reach for and hold a man when it was less physical than mental. Lew felt as though he was infinitely old and knowing. As though, by closing his eyes, he could trace out the precise pattern of everything that was now to flow out of the shooting of Smoky Buel, and that was what made him feel tired, because the old ways of violence seemed never to change, seemed confined within a rigid framework of cause and effect that neither he nor anyone else could alter at all.

"What about the trial now?" asked Ayers finally, turning his head almost languidly to stare out at Lew. "If Smoky can't testify, Sheriff, and there's more postponement, I want to be turned loose on bail."

"Yeah," said Lew dryly, "sure." He started back toward the door, passed through it, dropped the bar, and stood for a moment considering his coffee pot on the cold cook stove across the office.

"Damnation," he swore at the inoffensive coffee pot, crossed his office to the roadside door, and passed on out into the late night again.

It was pleasantly cool now. So cool, in fact, he knew it had to be around two or three o'clock in the morning. A glance up along the saloon hitch racks confirmed this; no saddled animals stood anywhere in view. Alturas was as quiet and still as the overhead sky except for some soft-falling footsteps coming on toward Main Street from the east. Lew remained in the formless dark under his jailhouse overhang until he saw a stroller come into view across the way and southward a few doors down. He stepped forth, went shagging on across to intercept that rusty shadow, and say: "Well, Doc, he's a gory mess isn't he?"

The medical man was young. Young enough in fact to be Lew Burton's son. He was taller than Lew but only half as broad and his boyish face was solemn now, and just a little bitter.

"You'd never guess what I was walking along here thinking, Sheriff," he said. "I was wondering why a man would stay in a place like this, when, if he had a lick of sense, he'd go back East and get into the maternity end of the medical field, leave all this sordidness to medical men who don't mind it. Who actually like it. There are doctors who do, you know."

"No," said Lew mildly, "I didn't know. But there's something I *do* know, Doc. Women havin' babies get a heap of help from Nature and men shot in the guts can die real easy if the medical men all hightail it at the first sight of messy gut shots."

The youthful doctor looked up at the empty, moonlighted roadway. He drew in a big sweeping gulp of good night air, and dropped his gaze with a wan smile back to Lew's face.

"You're right, of course," he said. "But it helps to vocally resent things sometimes."

"It helps every time," corrected Lew. "Sometimes I just saddle up, ride up into the hills, and lie in the shade hating mankind for all I'm worth. Then I can come back to town an' eat like a wolf an' sleep like a baby."

The doctor's lips parted, his eyes puckered, and he laughed. "You're pretty good medicine all by yourself," he said.

Lew did not comment; he'd winnowed the despair out and now he waited for what would come next, which was what he'd wanted to know in the first place.

"He'll be all right, Sheriff, but it was a mighty close call."

"Hit him from behind, didn't it?"

"Yes. From behind and pretty high up."

Lew's expression turned puzzled. "High up?"

"Yes, as though perhaps the ambusher was up a hillside or in a tree or something like that."

"But, hell," burst out Lew, "he was shot in the Halfmoon yard, which is as flat as the palm. . . ."

"Yes, Sheriff?"

"Nothing," muttered Lew. "Something just came to me, Doc. Well, you'll be wanting to get along home, I reckon. You'll look in on him, though, won't you?"

The doctor nodded. "As often as I can."

Lew inclined his head, stepped around the doctor, and walked slowly toward the hotel. In the loft, he told himself, that blasted back-shooter was up in the barn loft sure as the Lord made each new day. That was the only spot within rifle range, let alone carbine range, where anyone could shoot *down* at a man in Halfmoon's yard. The only plausible site of all.

Lew entered the lamp-lighted hotel lobby, which was entirely empty, crossed to the stairs, and went up them to his room. He entered, didn't bother to light his table lamp, and began to undress.

Something was troubling him. It was not at all impossible, since John Arnold had seen no one leaving Halfmoon as he rode in, that Smoky Buel's assassin had been in that loft all the while Lew was there. He may even have been up there with his sights fixed upon Buel's chest in the wagon, or John's head, or even Lew's own shoulder blades as he'd tooled that ranch wagon out of the yard.

He kicked off both boots, tossed aside his hat, shirt, and pants, then stood for a little while looking downward at Main Street.

Maybe he was getting old; a few more mistakes like that one, and, if he didn't wind up on a slab with a slug in his own back, someone would hear of it and the town council would replace him sure.

He went to bed, eased down tiredly, told himself from now on he would be more like he used to be, turned onto his side, and at once fell asleep.

IX

There was no hearing the following day. Lew was in with his prisoner, drinking coffee while Ayers ate a big breakfast, when Judge Harper came to the jail-house.

Harper stumped right on down the cell-block's dingy little corridor, scowled myopically in at Ayers, and said gruffly: "Lew, what's all this I hear about that cowboy witness being shot up last night at Halfmoon?"

"He's over at John Arnold's place," replied Sheriff Burton. "Someone ambushed him, Judge. Took him a pretty mean cut alongside the ribs with a carbine."

Harper peered owlishly in at Ayers again, swung his gaze back to Lew, and said: "Can he be in court today?"

Lew shook his head.

"I told you," said the judge almost accusingly, "I had to be over at Vegas for a trial tomorrow, Lew. Now I can't hang around here until you can get that man back on his feet, so you'll have to settle for a postponement."

"For how long, Judge?"

"Probably a week, maybe two weeks. I don't know for sure, but it'll be at least one week."

Mike Ayers spoke up. "Judge, how much is my bond?"

Harper squinted into the gloomy little cell again.

"Well," he said uncertainly, "can you stand a thousand dollars? If I set it any lower on a murder charge, people will holler their heads off."

"A thousand is fine," said Ayers, reaching into a pocket. "Sheriff . . ."—he nodded toward the locked steel door—"open up."

Lew did not move to obey. "For his own protection," he told Judge Harper, "he ought to stay in here. Whoever dry-gulched his pardner could do the same to him."

Before Harper could reply, Mike Ayers said dryly: "You're plumb wrong, Sheriff, plumb wrong." He had a fist full of bills in his hand that he pushed through at Sheriff Burton. "It's pretty hard to shoot a man who's expecting you to try it. Take the money, Sheriff, and let me out of here."

"Judge . . . ?" Lew began.

Harper screwed his face up indignantly. "What's the matter with you, Lew?" he snapped. "You know perfectly well this man's entitled to his freedom under bond. What're you trying to pull here?"

"I'm trying to prevent a war," retorted Lew acidly. "Ayers here thinks it was Flying E that shot his pardner. The minute he posts bond and straps on his gun there's going to be all hell bust loose."

Judge Harper looked in at Ayers again. "But he's entitled to post bond," he told Lew Burton. "If it'll help any, I'll have him put under a peace bond."

Lew snorted. "The difference between gun law an' book law," he growled, "is that book law doesn't work until someone has pulled a trigger. Then, usually, for someone it's too late. Your peace bond wouldn't be worth the paper it's printed on, Judge." Lew bent, inserted a key, and fiercely twisted it. "All right, Clarence," he said to the judge, "you said turn him loose, and, by golly, there he is . . . turned loose.

Now, when you get back from Vegas, you'll see what you've done."

"I don't make the law, Lew, and regardless of how right you may be, you can't change it."

Mike Ayers counted out $1,000 into Sheriff Burton's hand, nodded at the two older men, and strode on out into the sheriff's front office. There, he waited for his gun.

The judge left, and Lew reluctantly returned Ayers's six-gun. He dropped down at his desk to make out the bail receipt, and, as he did this, he said: "Listen, Ayers, Smoky told me you'd likely import some friends to help you salt down Flying E." Lew signed his name with a flourish to the receipt, handed it over, and motioned Ayers to the cane-bottomed chair beside his desk. "Don't do it, don't bring any gun hands to Washoe County. Maybe I can't expect you to let the law handle the shooting of Smoky Buel, but I'll tell you this . . . the day you ride into Alturas with a gun crew behind you, I'll deputize the whole blessed county if I have to, and lock up the lot of you."

Mike silently sat down, opened the gate of his six-gun, spun the cylinder to check the loads, closed the gate, and holstered the weapon. Not until then did he raise his eyes to Burton.

"I didn't have in mind bringing in outsiders, Sheriff, unless Eagleton wants it that way. What I had in mind was meeting Eagleton face to face and man to man. I believe he was behind the shooting of Smoky Buel. I think you also believe that. But there's no proof, so we'll let that slide for now. What I want Eagleton for is framing me into jail and dang' near getting me hanged." Ayers stood up. He considered Lew for a moment before speaking again. "But in the end, Sheriff, when Eagleton and I settle up, you can say it was for Smoky, too. Now tell me . . . where is the Arnold place?"

Lew got up. "I'll take you over there . . . was goin' over to check on things myself."

They left the jailhouse together, stepped out into dazzling morning sunlight, and hiked along side-by-side. There were not as yet many people abroad. Up at the livery barn a potbellied hostler was raking the front roadway, and at the mercantile establishment across the way a clerk in a white shirt and pink sleeve garters was arranging his sidewalk display of corrugated scrub boards and buckets.

Amos Darren walked out of his building northward, flung a bucket of water over the earth by his roadside hitch rack to minimize the dust for a while, saw Lew and Mike Ayers fading out eastward from Main Street, and stood there a moment frowning after them.

Alturas seemed to come to life reluctantly on summer mornings. The only roadway traffic was one dusty top buggy heading northwest out of town. In it was Judge Harper.

John Arnold was leaving his house when Lew and Ayers turned in at the gate. He met them just below the porch steps, nodded, and said: "He seems a little worse this morning, but then I kind of expected that anyway. He had a lot of jostling yesterday."

"Mind if we go in?" asked the sheriff.

Arnold shook his head, and stepped aside. "Evvie's feeding him. I've got to get the type set for the paper, but, as soon as I can, I'll hunt up Doc and send him down for another look."

John considered Mike Ayers from head to toe.

Ayers had kept quiet up to now but his steady gaze was gravely upon the newspaperman. "Any charge for your inconvenience," he told Arnold, "I'll be glad to pay."

John was briefly silent. He absently nodded his head, shot Lew Burton a look, then said to Mike: "I think I'll print the bill in my paper and address it to Flying E, not you."

Lew groaned. "Damn you, John," he said. "Last night you told me you weren't going to. . . ."

"Not today," interrupted Arnold. "Not until I'm certain Eagleton was behind the shooting of Buel. Don't worry, Lew."

"No," said Burton acidly, "I won't."

He and Ayers went on into the house. Evelyn met them in the parlor and Lew introduced her to Mike Ayers. Something very sudden and very electric came into the parlor atmosphere as those two stood gazing at one another. At first this annoyed Lew, then it embarrassed him. He growled something about wishing to see the wounded man to distract Evelyn Arnold, then followed her to where Smoky was lying. There, the way Ayers fixed his full attention upon Buel made Lew doubt that what had passed back and forth between Ayers and Evelyn Arnold out in the parlor had actually happened.

"Fine thing," said Ayers banteringly, his voice soft, his eyes probing. "Leave you alone for a few minutes and you run into a bullet backward. How do you feel, Smoky?"

Buel didn't look good but his spirit was strong. He said: "Well, Mike, in order to die I'd have to feel better."

Ayers looked solemnly over at Evelyn. "Beats all

what some men'll do just to get to loaf around in bed, ma'am."

Smoky's color improved under the prodding of this kind of rough range humor. He watched his partner and John Arnold's beautiful daughter exchange that solemn long look, and hung fire over whatever it was he had in mind to say, his eyes suddenly widening, turning wise and thoughtful. He and Lew Burton exchanged a glance.

"Find out yet who downed me, Sheriff?" Smoky asked, breaking that other spell at bedside with this soft-drawled question.

Lew straightened up off the footboard, shaking his head. "A man has to sleep sometime," he said sarcastically. "Were you lookin' for a miracle?"

"No, just a little piece of someone's hide." Smoky rolled his head on the pillow, looked at Mike Ayers, and said: "Maybe we'd ought to get back up to the ranch. I don't cotton to the notion of puttin' these folks out by cluttering up their house, Mike."

Evelyn put a hand upon Smoky's shoulder. "You're not going anywhere for a long time," she said, removed the hand, and looked straight over at Mike. "Please don't let him talk you into moving him."

"I wouldn't think of it," said Ayers, straightening up to his full height. He and Evelyn continued to look at one another for moments after he'd said this, until Smoky, looking intently from one of them to the other, screwed up his face at Sheriff Burton.

"I'll be darned," he said very clearly.

Ayers looked down. Lew saw faint color come beating into his lean, handsome face, and put up a hand to scratch the tip of his nose. Lew's eyes were beginning to twinkle. That electricity in the sick-room air was thick enough now to lean into. He glanced slyly from the corner of his eye at Evelyn; she was a little pink in the face, too. Lew dropped his hand, broadly grinned down at Buel, who didn't grin back. He looked just a tiny bit disgusted. Then Lew twirled his hat.

"Maybe we'd better be moving along," he said to Mike. "Evvie'll have her work to do an' we're hold-ing things up."

Evelyn led them out of the bedroom. She and Mike passed on out, but Lew, bringing up the rear, paused at the door, twisted, and made that mischie-vous grin back at Buel. "How good's your percep-tion?" he softly asked.

"My what?" said Smoky, frowning.

"If a feller'd lit a match in here when those two were lookin' at one another, the whole blessed house would have blown up."

Smoky's face cleared, then turned ironic. "That badge you wear is the wrong shape, Sheriff. Instead of bein' a star, it should be shaped like a heart.

Lew chuckled. "Maybe she can take his mind off Flying E."

"If she does, she'll get him killed."

Lew's smile vanished as the wounded man in his bed looked accusingly at him. "Rest easy on that score," he said, becoming once more the lawman he was by trade and training. "If there's any killing going to happen, I aim to be on hand."

"Not unless you change a heap," growled Smoky. "Arnold told me this morning about that boner you pulled in court yesterday morning."

Lew's humor was entirely gone now. He was nettled and showed it. He stood a moment longer, looking back at Smoky, then quietly closed the door and walked on through to the parlor with his hat in one hand. It came to him as he stepped along that now was the time for him to ride to Flying E. Before Eagleton came to Alturas and before Ayers went back to Halfmoon. If he could keep those two at arm's length a little longer—long enough to lay down the law—a showdown might be avoided.

When he came into the parlor, Mike and Evelyn Arnold were standing by the street side door, quietly talking. He couldn't distinguish what was being said but he could very easily see how those two were looking at one another. It occurred to him that, if anything matured between those two, John would be mad as a hornet—his daughter and a common gunfighter.

Lew crushed on his hat. Sometimes, no matter what a man did, he just couldn't win.

X

Ayers said he intended to talk to the doctor and remain in town for a few days, at least until he was certain Smoky was out of danger. That was all Lew wanted to be sure of before he got his horse from the livery barn and rode out into the cool of the morning, bound for Flying E.

It was not as far to Cyrus Eagleton's place as it was to Halfmoon, and this distance was in fact the basic difference between those two outfits. Where Halfmoon had the Horseshoe Hills to shade its grass, store its water, and shelter its range from winter's blasts, Flying E was almost entirely out upon the alkali plains. Even the main ranch buildings were unrelieved by trees as was also the case at Halfmoon. Flying E looked exactly like what it was—a functional cow ranch with none of the blessings that in desert Nevada made the difference between hard living and good living.

There was one huge old barn weathered bone-gray, a number of outbuildings such as a smithy, storehouse, harness shack, and bunkhouse, then there was the part-log, part-adobe main ranch house where Eagleton lived. Taken altogether, Flying E was a man's world. Cy Eagleton, like many men of his kind through the West, had never married. As Sheriff Burton approached, with the sun beginning to burn across his shoulders, he thought for the hundredth time that what this ranch needed was trees, some greenery to relieve the eternal alkali dust—in short, Flying E needed a woman's touch.

That thought always, in retrospect, brought a hard smile to Lew's lips, because of all the cowmen he knew, Cyrus Eagleton, the rough, conniving, transplanted Texan, was the last man he could imagine who would be either influenced by a woman, or who would take one seriously.

He passed through a square block of barn shade, swung half around toward the main house, and met Lefty Doolin emerging from the barn. Doolin didn't look surprised but he halted in his tracks at the sight of the sheriff.

Lew swung down, looped his reins where a stud ring hung from a barn balk, nodded at Doolin, and said: "Mister Eagleton over at the main house?"

Doolin's answer came slowly; he was obviously curious about what had brought the law to Flying E. "As far as I know, he is. But he's fixin' to head for town for the trial."

"No trial today," said Lew, and started on across the yard conscious that Flying E's foreman was staring a hole in his back.

He was still fifty feet off when Eagleton stepped out of his house, closed the door, and stood there in verandah shade, watching his approach. Eagleton did not nod and Lew thought that, if that was the way Eagleton wanted it, that would be fine with him. He stopped just short of the verandah with hot sunlight upon him and said: "No trial today, so you can save yourself a ride."

Eagleton's expression did not change. He nodded though. "Too bad you had to ride so far to tell us," he said, still watching Lew with a blank face.

"I didn't have to tell you," said Lew. "In fact, as far

as I'm concerned, I'd have let the lot of you ride into town and find out for yourselves except for one thing."

"Yeah?" said Eagleton, his face hardening against Burton for Lew's bluntness. "What's that?"

"Mike Ayers is out on bail."

Eagleton looked on over the yard where Lefty Doolin and several other Flying E riders were lounging by the barn. He coldly smiled. "Is that supposed to scare us, Sheriff?" he scornfully asked. "Because if it is . . . it's a flop."

Lew let that go by. He hooked both thumbs in his shell belt and said: "I came out here to give you some advice, Mister Eagleton. Keep Flying E out of Alturas for a few days."

"Why?"

Lew kept his voice quiet as he told of the shooting of Smoky Buel, but it wasn't easy because at once he saw the faint smirk light up Cy Eagleton's hawkish features.

"That's too bad," murmured Eagleton, when Lew finished speaking. "An' he was Ayers's only supportin' witness, too."

"I didn't say he was killed," growled Lew. "I said he was shot . . . wounded."

"But wounded men got a way of dyin', Sheriff."

That was a threat or a promise and Lew took it that way. He began to get mad. From behind him on across the yard Lefty Doolin called lazily up to the main house.

"Anythin' special this mornin', Cy?"

Eagleton's smirk lingered when he called back: "Naw, nothing special now, Lefty! No trial in town an' the law'll be ridin' on pretty quick, then we can get a little fresh air around here."

From over by the barn came the taunting laughter of several Texas cowhands.

Lew had a struggle of it to keep his anger in check. He had never run into this solid arrogance in Cyrus Eagleton before. But then, he'd never before crossed him, either. Now he began disliking Eagleton in a way he'd seldom disliked anyone before.

"Anything else, Sheriff?" drawled the lank cowman from his position in the porch shade. "Because this is a workin' cow outfit an' we aren't like some folks . . . we can't go sportin' around the countryside on other folks' money."

"One other thing," said Lew, his lips drawn out thin but otherwise showing no anger. "I want a word or two with Turk Mahoney."

"Turk? Well, that's sure too bad, Sheriff. Turk's not here."

"No? You knew he'd have to testify in court this morning."

Eagleton shrugged. "Then maybe it's just as well there's to be no trial, because I sent Turk out to a desert line camp last night."

Lew looked over at Eagleton, saw in the Texan's arrogant expression that this was a lie and that Eagleton knew Lew knew it was a lie, and was standing there now, daring Lew to say so. When Lew remained silent, Eagleton smiled.

"Tell you what, Sheriff," he drawled. "When Turk comes back, I'll send him to see you. How's that for co-operation?"

Lew ignored the question. It was in his mind to put out a few feelers about the ambushing of Smoky Buel now, but before he got the chance Eagleton spoke again.

"But as for Flying E stayin' out of Alturas . . . can't

oblige you there, Burton. But even if we didn't have
business in town, we'd still have more right there
than that two-bit gunfighter has." Eagleton paused,
half turned to reënter the house, then said as an af-
terthought: "By the way . . . you didn't say who shot
that Buel feller." He gazed out at Lew, slowly smiled,
and said: "Or don't you know who shot him?"

Lew's anger was turning his face pale in spite of
the heat. He said softly: "I haven't any idea who shot
Buel. Whoever he was, he did it from ambush." An
idea came to Lew; without considering it at all he
acted upon it, saying: "Ayers is leaving Buel in town
until he recovers, but he'll be heading back to the
Halfmoon today, probably, to stay there by himself
until Buel can come back, then they'll have their
cattle work to do."

Eagleton looked steadily out at Lew for a moment
as though he was carefully sifting those words. Finally he inclined his head, said—"See you again,
Sheriff."—and walked on into the house.

Lew stood still a second or two, viewing that
closed door before he turned and went walking
stiffly back toward his horse. He'd known when he'd
come out here that he had no legal grounds supporting his wish to keep Flying E out of Alturas, but he
hadn't expected to find Eagleton so thoroughly an-
tagonistic, either.

Lefty Doolin stepped up and handed Lew his
reins. Doolin was wearing that same contemptuous
smile he'd turned on Mike Ayers after the trial in
Alturas the day before. "Have a nice ride back," he
murmured to Lew. Behind Doolin several lounging
riders broadly smiled at that remark.

Lew took the reins, stepped up over leather, and
reined away, his face white to the eyes. It had been

many years since Lew Burton had been as thoroughly mad as he was on the ride back to town.

He had only one thought to alleviate that anger. When he'd told Eagleton that Mike Ayers was going back to Halfmoon, he'd acted upon a hunch. The closer he got to Alturas the more he concentrated upon this. By the time he rode in at the livery barn with blazing, breathless early afternoon all around him, he had the details of his hunch fairly well worked out.

He sought Mike Ayers at the boarding house, at the jail, even at John Arnold's house, and found him at none of those places. Where he finally did find him was the last place it would have occurred to him to look. As he was striding northward along the east side of Main Street past the *Clarion*'s office, he automatically looked in, and there sat Mike Ayers and John Arnold at John's littered desk, sharing a bucket of beer.

Lew entered, wagged his head over this unlikely association, made no comment about it, and dragged up a chair. John rummaged for a third glass, carefully poured it full of tepid beer, and pushed it over at Lew. Mike sat there viewing Lew's sweaty shirt, saying nothing.

"We've been speculating," said Arnold to the sheriff, his tone easy, his words conversational, and his expression showing no hint that only two days earlier he had fiercely castigated the very man he was now visiting with, "about which one of Eagleton's crew shot Buel. What's your guess, Lew?"

"Guessing about things like that never much interested me," said Lew crisply. "I leave that to you, John." He looked at Mike, related what had passed out at Flying E, then said: "Eagleton may think that you're going up to Halfmoon today. I sort of gave him that idea."

"I told you," retorted Ayers a little coldly, "I was going to hang around town for a few days."

"I know. Maybe I had no right to tell Eagleton that, but if you'll step over to my office for a few minutes, I'll explain what occurred to me at Eagleton's place."

Ayers made no move to rise. He took up his glass, drank, set the glass down, and said: "Tell me right here, Sheriff."

John Arnold began to look darkly at Lew. He was, Lew saw, on the verge of making one of his angry tirades, so Lew spoke out quickly, ahead of this approaching outburst. "All right. John, if you breathe a word of this, you just might get someone shot."

"Breathe a word of what," demanded Arnold, glaring. "Lew, when have I ever . . . ?"

"Never mind," interrupted Lew. "Now listen, you two. The man who shot Buel was in the hayloft of Halfmoon's barn." He paused as both Arnold and Ayers looked over at him, their glances mirroring surprise and quick interest.

"Doc gave me that information accidentally last night when he told me how the slug came angling downward when it hit Buel. There's no other high place for a man to hide at Halfmoon to shoot at that angle."

"Wait a minute," said Arnold suddenly. "Lew, I didn't see anyone leaving when I rode in only moments after Buel was shot."

The significance of what he'd said showed clearly in John Arnold's face. He was thinking exactly what Lew had already surmised, that the assassin had had no chance to escape after the shooting, that in all probability he had still been in that loft when Arnold and Sheriff Burton were there.

Lew nodded. Mike Ayers, left out of this exchange, looked from one man to the other, frowning. "Is this some state secret," he asked, "or can an outsider hear it, too?"

Lew explained, Mike listened, his interest steadily heightened until he was sitting straight up in his chair. "All right," he eventually said. "What's in your mind, Sheriff?"

"I'm guessing now, but if Eagleton did have a hand in Buel's shooting, and if he really wants you out of the way, I left the way wide open for him to put that same assassin back into the Halfmoon loft again tonight."

Lew leaned back, picked up his beer glass, sipped from it, and watched John Arnold and Mike Ayers digest this part of his impromptu plan. He was putting the glass back on the table when Ayers finally spoke.

"All right, Sheriff, you've set me up for the target. I'll go along with you."

Lew said: "Good. We'd better get going."

"Wait a minute," Ayers retorted. "Not we, Sheriff, me. I'll ride up alone. If there's anything to this, let's assume Eagleton will also have men watching to see whether or not I actually return to Halfmoon, and whether or not I return alone."

John Arnold wagged his head. "Man," he told Ayers, "there's just one thing wrong with this plan . . . you could damned easily get killed."

Ayers arose. "Not as easily as you think, Mister Arnold. I didn't come down in the last rain." He looked over at Lew. "What's the rest of your plan?"

"I'll ride up after dark. You'd better not ride into

the yard until I've had a chance to get up there, too. Give me until dark to get into position, then ride into the barn and stay in there. If our man's in the loft, he'll wait for you to walk across toward the house, with your back to him like Buel's was."

Arnold erupted. "You're crazy," he said excitedly to Lew Burton. "You're going to get this man killed, Lew."

Burton also got up. He shook his head at the newspaperman. "He'll stay in the barn, John. When I get up there, I'll get into the barn, too. No one will walk out into the yard. Do you understand?"

Arnold looked straight at Burton and said: "Lew, this is crazy."

XI

John Arnold protested a little more but Mike Ayers appeared adamant. He finished his beer, left the *Clarion*'s office, and a little later Lew and John saw him ride out of town northward at a leisurely gait.

John eased himself back in his chair after Mike was no longer in view and put a bleak stare over at the sheriff. "He's a fool to go along with that plan of yours, Lew," Arnold grumbled. "Look, suppose Eagleton doesn't aim to have him shot like Buel got it, suppose as soon as he rides up into those dog-gone hills Eagleton sends a man or two down to dry-gulch him before he even gets close to the ranch?"

Lew said: "That possibility exists, John, I'll admit it, and I also considered it. But you're overlookin' Ayers. He's no novice. Anyone who tries to bush-whack him will get one hell of a surprise."

"You don't know that, Lew."

"No, and I don't know Eagleton will try to have him killed, either. But this will prove two things I need to know. One, whether or not Cy Eagleton really was behind that attempted killing of Buel. And, two, whether or not Mike can take care of himself."

Arnold looked at the empty bucket on his desk, leaned far over, and peered into it to make certain all the beer was gone. It was, so he leaned back again, saying: "You're sure pickin' a hard way to find those things out."

Lew got up. "Sure am," he assented succinctly, and started for the door.

"Where you going now?" asked Arnold.

"Over to your house to see Buel, then, when it's a little darker, on up to Halfmoon."

He left the newspaper office, squinted at the brassy sky, started south toward the first intersecting roadway, checked himself, turned, and hiked off in a fresh direction, this time bound for the combination residence-office of the doctor. It was an off chance that he'd find the medical man at home, but he took it anyway, and he won. The doctor was writing in his anteroom when Lew walked in. He looked up, nodded without smiling, pushed aside his writing materials, and motioned Lew to a little chair.

"You look dehydrated," he said, making a correct prognosis from Lew's appearance. "Look like a man who's been out in the sun too long."

"In weather like this ten minutes is too long. Tell me, Doc, how's our patient?"

The doctor lifted his shoulders and let them fall. "Better," he said. "He's tough, otherwise we might have trouble."

"From the busted ribs?"

"No, from the loss of blood." The doctor evidently thought of something, for his face brightened. "It's funny what a morale builder it is for ailing men to have pretty nurses. Buel insists on shaving himself and combing his own hair. I believe Miss Evelyn is better medicine that I could prescribe."

"Tell me again how that bullet struck him," said Lew.

"Well, as I told you, it came downward at him from behind."

"From a goodly height maybe, say, perhaps thirty, forty feet?"

"Yes, probably from as high as that. Why, Sheriff, does this tell you something about the man who fired that bullet?"

"Nothing about the man, Doc, but maybe something about where he was when he downed Buel."

"I see. Well, I can tell you this much. He wasn't very far off. That slug hadn't lost much momentum when it hit. Buel's flesh was ragged on the outside, but that was from the introduction of a foreign object beneath the skin, expanding and tearing it. But inside, in the muscles where it passed through, it made a cut as neat as any slicing knife would have done. It was traveling extremely fast when it hit, and from that I'd say the assassin was not very far behind Buel when he fired."

Lew got up, struck his dusty trouser leg with his hat, and looked pleased. There were no trees, no outbuildings, nothing northward from Halfmoon's yard where a gunman could have concealed himself to ambush Smoky Buel—except that log barn.

"You've been a great help," he told the medical man. "I'm obliged to you, Doc. Now, one more question . . . is it all right for Buel to have visitors?"

"Sure, Sheriff, just don't tire him out. What he needs is rest, sleep, and lots of food. Time and his outdoorsman's constitution will do the rest."

Lew left the doctor's place, paused on the yonder sidewalk to consider the off-center sun again, and went along to his office. There, he made his afternoon cup of coffee, stripped off his shirt, poured a basin full of water, and washed himself from the waist up. Afterward, feeling not only cleaner, but fresher and cooler, he selected a Winchester from his rifle rack, methodically loaded it, stood it by the door, filled his pockets with extra cartridges, and sat down at his desk for a brief rest.

He was still sitting there when the afternoon shadows began flying downward from the far-away hills, and, when Evelyn Arnold walked in, he was chewing an unlighted cigar, looking thoughtfully pleased, and also drowsy.

Evelyn brought his eyes wide open. "Anything wrong?" he asked swiftly, studying the beautiful girl's face.

"Nothing," she said, going toward that old cane-bottomed chair. "At least not with Smoky. But I just looked in on Dad and he told me Mike has gone back up to his ranch."

Lew's face turned a little flinty. "He tell you anything else, Evvie?" he asked.

"No. Wasn't that enough, Uncle Lew? Why did you let him go up there?" Evelyn's liquid large eyes were accusing. "Whoever tried to kill Smoky might be waiting."

"Now, honey, don't you worry any about Mike Ayers. He's been in tighter places than this. No one's going to drop him from ambush."

"Will you do me a favor, Uncle Lew? Will you ride up there and make certain of that?"

Lew slowly nodded and slowly smiled. "I didn't know it could happen that fast," he murmured. "You like him, don't you, Evvie?"

There was no embarrassment, no false modesty showing in Evelyn Arnold's face as she nodded.

"Tell me something, Evvie. As a lifelong bachelor I've often wondered about this. What is it in a man that makes a woman like him when she doesn't even know what he's like? When all she's heard of him is bad or half bad?"

Evelyn remained mute for a long time. She looked away from Lew, then back again. She very faintly smiled, this smile turning her face sweet, turning it tender. "I don't think I can define it, Uncle Lew. It's something a woman feels. Something. . . ." She made a little fluttery gesture and dropped her hands. "I can't explain it and I don't suppose men feel it at all."

Lew's eyes twinkled. "Don't you be too sure of that," he said. "When he first laid eyes on you, I could see the change come over him. He felt something. For a while there in the parlor I thought he was going to embarrass all of us an' say something personal. No, honey, Mike Ayers stepped into something he won't find it easy to step out of, when he walked into your parlor this morning. I may know nothin' about womenfolks, but I know men like a book." Lew paused, put his head a little to one side, made a wise and raffish little grin, and concluded with: "And when I got back to town, you know where your Mike Ayers was? In your pa's office with a bucket of beer, sittin' there visitin' your dad like John hadn't just flayed him the day before in an editorial."

"Dad told me. He said Mike wasn't at all like he'd thought he'd be."

"Sure not," retorted Lew. "A man like Mike Ayers can be downright charming when he wants to be, and I'd guess, because you're John's daughter, he wanted to be. Now I'm not saying he isn't a decent enough young feller, Evvie. I think he probably is. What I'm sayin' is that the same bug bit him that bit you and he's layin' a little groundwork before he asks your pa if it's all right for him to call on you."

Evelyn got up. She looked solemnly down at Lew and said: "I hope you're right, Uncle Lew. And I hope nothing happens to him up at Halfmoon. You won't forget that favor, will you?"

Lew pushed up out of his chair. He felt almost young again. "I'll keep an eye out for him," he promised. "And you do the same for Smoky."

After Evelyn left, Lew stood a moment in thought. It did not now appear likely that John Arnold would be angry, after all, when he discovered that Evelyn was interested in Mike Ayers. He reached for the loaded Winchester, re-settled the hat upon his head, and stepped out into afternoon's soft-saffron shadings with an almost jaunty step. Sometimes it was just plain good to be alive.

He paused for a look northward at the bare and shadowy Horseshoe Hills, some of his exuberance left but not all of it as he considered what might lie ahead, then he struck out for the livery barn.

Ed Grosson was leaving the bank. He turned slowly at sight of Lew, walking along with that cradled carbine, followed Lew into the barn with his gaze, then hastened to lock the bank's double doors and cross over after Lew.

John Arnold had also seen Lew walking along with that Winchester in his arms, but John was looking out his office window and he made no move to leave this spot. He simply ran an ink-stained set of stubby fingers through his scanty hair and dolorously wagged his head back and forth. John knew how tough Lew Burton could be; he also surmised that Mike Ayers would be a hard man to whip. But he'd lived for quite a number of years within the shadow of Cy Eagleton's Flying E, too, and he had no illusions about what might ensue when those three forces met head-on in a violent clash.

The liveryman was saddling and bridling Lew's animal when Grosson entered the barn, spied Lew halfway down through runway gloom, and went over to him to say: "What's up, Sheriff. I saw that you'd turned Ayers loose this morning. Any more trouble in the making?"

Lew looked at the banker's inquisitive, slightly troubled face. "Maybe yes and maybe no," he said. "It's too early to say, Ed, but you've got nothing to worry about anyway. No one's going to rob your safe as far as I know, which is your particular headache."

"That's not my only headache," retorted Grosson a trifle sharply, "and you know it." Lew's unconcern, his almost jovial mood, irritated Grosson. "If it isn't trouble, how come you to be ridin' out with a rifle?"

"Varmints," said Lew solemnly. "The countryside's full of 'em lately." He took his horse, poked the carbine into its saddle boot, swung up, and touched his hat brim to Grosson. "Have a good supper, Ed," he said, and rode out.

A number of people watched Sheriff Burton ride out of Alturas. Some of them were still watching when he left the road a mile out, swung westerly, and booted his beast over into a slow canter. He wasn't at that time heading for the Horseshoe Hills at all; he was riding almost parallel. John Arnold was the only watcher who understood what Lew was doing, and John kept his own council. He returned to his composing table, adjusted the lamp there, tilted forward his green eyeshade, and went back to work. He was still setting type almost an hour later when he heard a rushing body of horsemen clatter down Main Street from out of the gathering dusk, turned, pushed up his eyeshade, and peered out into the roadway.

The first rider John saw clearly enough to recognize was Lefty Doolin. The second one was hawkish Cy Eagleton. The others, swinging down across the road in front of a saloon, were all Flying E cowboys.

John lifted his apron, methodically wiped his hands, and walked slowly over to his roadside front window. There, he watched that dark and bunched-up body of rough men tie their animals to the rail, toss words back and forth, then step around to the plank walk, scuff across it, and push on into the saloon all in a body.

John's initial reaction to the sight of Flying E in town was uneasiness, but the longer he stood there at his window watching those Texans, the more relieved he became. Lew and Mike Ayers would have a long ride for nothing now, he told himself, but at least they'd survive to ride back again, which was something he was not sure they'd have been able to do if Flying E was up there waiting for them in the hills.

John started to turn away from his window. A passer-by swung into view, looked in at John, and slowed. It was big Amos Darren. They exchanged a nod, then Amos entered the office, closed the door, and said: "Eagleton just hit town. It's a damned good thing Ayers isn't around. It looked like he had his whole crew with him."

"Yeah," said John, "I saw them. They're across the road at the bar."

"I suppose," said Darren, "Lew'll hear of their arrival."

"Lew's not in town."

Darren's steady gaze remained upon Arnold for a while as he thought on this information, then he shrugged, reached behind him for the doorknob, and said: "Well, as long as it's just Flying E, I reckon the worst we can expect is some shot-out road lights and maybe a few busted windows. We'll survive, Lew or no Lew. We've survived before."

John leaned across his composing table, looking at big Amos. "What happens when they accidentally kill someone, Amos, maybe a woman or a kid or a stranger passing through?"

Darren grunted, opened the door a crack, and said: "Yeah. I've wondered about that, too. Lew said somethin' to me yesterday that sort of made me mad, but he was right, John. He said we wouldn't do anything about Flying E because we like Eagleton's money too well."

"That'd make a good editorial, Amos."

Darren squinted his eyes at John. "It'd make an obituary, too, John, if you wrote it an' Eagleton read it." Darren walked out, and closed the door.

XII

There were times when something sparked a man's good nature and nothing could dampen it again, not even personal peril. That was the way Lew Burton rode through the gathering shadows. He felt good about something. Evvie had started it back in Lew's office, but feeling fresh and clean also helped. Then, too, there was a silvery moon overhead in a purple-enamel sky, a wide rash of white-cold stars, and the day's long period of suffocating heat was past. All of these things worked their will upon Lew, keeping him feeling in good spirits.

He passed on into the hills west of Halfmoon, rode north for a while, then, where the junipers thickened and a scent of water brought his mount's ears up, he swung back southward and a little eastward. In this manner, riding in out of the dark-layered night, he came along a narrow cañon between two bare hills and into the upper end of Halfmoon's home ranch pasture.

He encountered scattered bands of cattle, some greasy fat and dark red, some rough-coated, gaunt, and bleached-out-looking. He also came upon a little band of loose horses. The cattle didn't pay him much attention, but the horses did; they threw up their tails like plumes and went careening away. Lew smiled and paced along. The night was warm, the air tart with an acid scent from creosote bush and blue lupine, and until he could distantly make out Halfmoon's unlighted, darkly square, low buildings, he rocked along loosely in the saddle and unmindfully. After that sighting, though, he lost the looseness and the comfortable languidness.

A half mile out he stopped, got down, and stood at his horse's head while both of them listened and looked. The silence hanging over this big, hushed land was limitless. Lew walked ahead for a way, leading his animal. He came upon a segment of that old post-and-rider fence Pete Frazier had laboriously built many decades before. Here, he sought a particularly shadowy place, tied his horse beyond any accidental finding, snaked out the Winchester, and went along again, staying always within the gloomy shadows of that old wooden fence.

Halfmoon's gaunt old barn stood out darker than the night, its solidity a black square against a sooty horizon. It was so quiet, in close to the ranch yard. Without any knowledge where Eagleton was, or where he might be, Lew employed all his caution until, approaching the barn from the doorless and windowless north, he felt reasonably safe. At least from here, unless a man stepped boldly out and exposed himself, Lew was quite safe.

He stopped again, keening the night as an old lobo wolf might have done, testing it with his senses, before stepping away from the post-and-rider fence, starting swiftly across the intervening open distance to the first pole corrals where dingy shadows would again camouflage him with their alternating bars of black and gray. He was now less than 200 feet from the barn's easterly front opening. If he was right, Mike would be waiting in there. Also, if he was right, they'd have an assassin trapped overhead in the loft. If he was wrong. . . .

Lew glided along the corral, reached the barn's rough, weathered north wall, paused a second, listening, then made it on around to within a few feet of the doorless big front opening. Not a sound came out of the barn. He rose up, balanced on the balls of his feet, jumped around, and landed down upon the hard earthen floor in total darkness. He was inside and presumably safe, but presumably was never good enough when a man had only one life to gamble with, so he took two large onward steps making no sound at all and finally halted well away from where he'd initially lit down.

No shot came; in fact, no sound at all came from around him, making him wonder whether or not he was alone in the barn. Moments passed. A little round stone struck softly close to Lew's right foot. Another little stone brushed against his shin. He shifted his hold of the Winchester, took several forward steps, came to the first tie stall, and looked over. The stall was empty. He moved along looking into each stall until, at the fifth one, he saw Mike standing perfectly motionless, watching him.

They came together in the darkness, exchanged a tight little nod, and Mike pointed upward with his thumb, nodded, and ran a finger across his throat, indicating that their assassin was, in fact, overhead in the loft.

Lew put his lips to the taller man's ear. "How do you know?" he whispered.

Mike bent close to answer. "Heard him on a rickety board up there. From the sound I'd say he's a pretty good-sized man, too. Maybe Eagleton himself."

Lew wagged his head at this. He knew Cy Eagleton too well to believe he'd do his own dirty work. He tried for a moment to guess which Flying E cowboy might be up there, but all Eagleton's men were lank. Some were heavier than others, but none was a small man. Then he gave this up; it wasn't important. What *was* important was getting that man alive if possible, so he could be made to talk, but if that wasn't possible, of getting the ambusher regardless. He twisted to look over where the loft ladder went up a wall. It was too dark to make that ladder out. He looked back at Mike.

Mike shook his head. "I did as you did, left my horse and slipped in here in the dark. For all he knows he's the only one in this barn."

"But they must've seen you ridin' up into the hills," said Lew, believing Eagleton would be concentrating upon this ambush and nothing else.

Mike shrugged. "I didn't see a soul on the way up. For that matter I didn't even find where our friend up there left his doggoned horse and I scouted around looking for the animal before I slipped in here, to make sure he was up there or not."

Again Lew looked over where the loft ladder was. He brushed Mike's arm and jerked his head. They stealthily left their tie stall, cat-footed it over to the barn's rough south wall, halted near the ladder, and looked upward where a square opening showed in the overhead planking. Lew stepped in close, bent his head until it almost touched those worn rungs, then stepped back again. He turned to nod strongly, indicating that he'd found where boots had roiled the dust as someone had climbed upward.

Mike put his head close to Lew's ear. "Let's give him a chance to come out peaceably," he said. "If he's got a lick of sense, he'll do it. He can't get out of there as long as we're down here. All we've got to do is wait him out. He'll figure those things out."

Lew nodded; he'd had something like that in mind. He motioned Mike to walk back a way, then he looked up at that dark overhead opening, and spoke forth.

"You up there in the loft, this is Sheriff Lew Burton of Alturas. Drop your weapons through the ladder hole and come down from up there!"

Lew waited, imagining the astonishment on the unseen assassin's face. When Mike stirred impatiently, Lew threw up an arm. That man up there would have some decisions to make and some surprise to get over. He couldn't be expected to do it all in a few seconds.

A full minute passed without any sound from the loft at all. Lew figured this was enough time so he called out again.

"You can't play 'possum up there, feller! We know you're up there, so make your play or we'll have to smoke you out."

Lew's echo came back mockingly, then it faded and the utter silence returned. "Listen," said the lawman, his tone turning sharp, "you toss your weapons down and no one suffers. Try something else and you'll live to regret it. You can't get out except the way you got up there. No one's going to come along in time to help you . . . and we're not going to wait all night for you to realize these things. Now, either spit or close the window!"

This time Lew got action. Overhead some boards groaned as a man's considerable weight shifted, but for another long moment there was no answer to the lawman's challenges. Finally though a man's gruff voice said: "All right, I'll come down, but tell your posse men to hold their fire."

"Toss down the guns first," ordered Lew.

A carbine dropped down, struck hard-packed earth, and clattered. Seconds later a six-gun also fell through that overhead square crawl hole.

"Now you," said Lew, "and keep both hands on the rungs."

They saw the man begin his descent but it was too dark to identify him until he paused near the bottom, still several feet off the ground, twisted his head around, and looked right and left for his captors. Then he completed his descent and turned, placing his heavy shoulders to the ladder.

Lew looked and said, sounding surprised: "Mahoney!"

The cowboy swung a little toward Burton's voice. Lew stepped up where he could be seen, still holding his Winchester.

"Turk Mahoney." Lew closed his mouth, shook his head disbelievingly, looked around as Mike Ayers came up beside him, looked back at the squinting, silent prisoner, and swore softly.

"I guess being wrong about a man sours a feller on other men. Turk, I've known you a long time. I never had you pegged for a back-shooter. I thought you were rough and maybe a little wild now and then . . . but a dry-gulcher, no."

Mahoney stood there as though carved from wood. He stared past Lew at Mike Ayers, saying nothing. He gradually swung his head looking around the barn, and eventually he said: "Where are the others?"

"What others?"

"You kep' saying *we* when you called me down."

Now Mike spoke. "He thought you had a posse with you, Lew. It might puncture his self-esteem if he knows there are only two of us."

Mahoney's eyes jumped to Mike's face and stayed there. "That's all?" he asked. "Just the two of you?"

"That's enough!" the sheriff exclaimed. "For your kind, Turk, either one of us is enough. Where's Eagleton?"

"I don't know. I come up here alone."

"Like you did the last time, eh?"

"If you're talking about that Buel feller, guess again. I didn't shoot him."

"Who did?"

Mahoney shook his head at the sheriff, his confidence returning. "I didn't," he said again, and left it like that.

Mike Ayers, studying Mahoney, stepped back, scooped up Mahoney's six-gun where it lay nearby, spun the cylinder, moved over, and dropped the weapon back into Mahoney's hip holster. He brushed Lew aside with his left hand, backed off twenty feet, and stopped, wide-legged, directly in front of the prisoner. He gently nodded.

"Any time," he said.

Lew was ten feet to one side of those two. He had not understood what Ayers was up to right away. Now, although he understood plainly enough, he was not foolish enough to move forward. In a fraction of a second one or the other of those two might draw and fire. Lew didn't move; he didn't even speak. Sometimes distractions were fatal to the people who diverted a gunman's attention.

Mahoney stood there, staring straight out at Ayers. It was obvious to Lew, who'd faced many gunmen, that this delay was fatal to Mahoney's courage and

his resolve. When a gunfighter thought too long before going into action, he lost his nerve.

"Come on," said Ayers softly. "I'm giving you a
better break than you figured to give me. Make your
play."

Mahoney finally moved; he stiffly shook his head
at Mike. "No. I've seen you draw, Ayers. I'm not going
to draw on you."

Mike did not relax; he, too, was experienced in
this kind of a meeting. No one threw him off guard.
He'd seen others turn away at the wrong time and
die through treachery.

"Then I'll kill you anyway, Mahoney, unless you
speak up. Who shot Buel?"

Lew saw Mahoney's lips turn loose, saw his eyes
waver. "Doolin," he whispered, and the second he'd
named that name self-loathing showed in his expression.

"Why?"

"For money."

"Let's have it from the start," demanded Mike Ayers, still standing ready.

"Eagleton offered five hundred to anyone who'd
down Buel and a thousand to anyone who'd down
you."

Ayers was briefly silent, his face showing contempt.
"Take his gun, Lew," he said to the sheriff, and, when
Mahoney was again disarmed, Ayers gradually
straightened up again.

Lew was between them when he said: "Turk, why
didn't Doolin try for the thousand? Why was he
content to go for Buel at five hundred?"

"He wasn't. He wanted both jobs, but Eagleton
said no, he said this time Doolin was to be around
where folks could see him. You asked a while back

where Eagleton was. The whole crew exceptin' me rode into town tonight."

"Why not you?"

Mahoney lifted a big arm, wiped sweat from his face, and dropped his arm. "Eagleton told you I was out at a line camp. All of us was goin' to swear to that so I'd have a real good alibi."

Lew heard Mike let off a long breath behind him. He stepped away from Mahoney, turned, and looked at the gunfighter, saw the scorn and bitterness in Ayers's face, and gestured toward the barn's front opening. "Let's get out of here," he said. "Where's your horse, Mahoney?"

"Hid over behind the main house," replied the prisoner, moving out after the sheriff, stepping past Mike Ayers and woodenly avoiding his stare.

XIII

It was past midnight when they got back to Alturas. Perhaps it was the lateness of the hour or possibly it was the silence they rode through all the way down out of the Horseshoe Hills, but neither Lew Burton nor Mike Ayers had anything to say until they were in Lew's office with their captive.

Lew lit the lamp, poked up a fire in his little cook stove, set the coffee pot on to boil, crossed over to his desk, and put Mahoney's six-gun there. Ayers dropped down in the cane-bottomed chair, thrust his legs far out, tilted his head back, and put an assessing look upward where Mahoney stood awkwardly watching Lew and waiting.

"Sit down," said Lew without looking around at Mahoney. "I want it in writing this time, Turk. You tell me again about that ambushing arrangement you and Lefty Doolin had with Eagleton, how much he agreed to pay you boys, and all the details. Talk slow because I got to write it all down. When I'm finished, you sign it."

Lew twisted to look up. Mahoney swung his eyes to a wired-together chair, went after the thing, and sat down upon it. He looked very carefully at his two hands as he began speaking. Until he finished he did not look at either Sheriff Burton or Mike Ayers, but then he did, and his expression had that same self-loathing look to it Mahoney had had in the Halfmoon barn.

All around the three of them Alturas slumbered. There were a few night lights burning, but otherwise the town could have been deserted, it was so still and empty-appearing.

Lew's pen scratched over paper, Mahoney's chair *creaked* under his solid weight, somewhere not far off in a tree a barn owl made its mournful cry. Mike Ayers sat there like a stone watching Mahoney.

"How much did Eagleton pay you to change your testimony about how that fight started when you and that other Flying E man rode to my ranch to break down the pasture fence?" Ayers asked.

Mahoney looked swiftly up and swiftly down. "A hundred dollars," he mumbled.

Ayers nodded very gently at Mahoney. "You're pretty hungry, aren't you, Turk?"

Mahoney fell to studying his hands again and Lew finished writing, pushed the transcript over, and poked the pen at him. "Sign right there on the last page," he ordered. "Mike, you'll witness it."

"Eagleton'll challenge that," said Ayers. "Might be better if you went and rousted a couple of townsmen out of bed to witness it, Lew."

"The hell with that," growled Burton, taking back the pen from Mahoney. "When this town starts doubtin' my word and my handwritin', they can get themselves another lawman." He held the pen toward Ayers, who took it, shrugged, and signed.

As Ayers finished signing, he lifted his head, sniffed, and swung to look over at the stove. Lew saw this, let out a squawk, and sprang up. His coffee was boiling over.

Mahoney watched the sheriff try to salvage his coffee pot and for the first time in many hours he smiled. Lew was more concerned over his ruined brew than over the implications involved in that signed confession upon his desk.

Mike Ayers, too, smiled a little. He waited until Lew had returned to his desk in titanic disgust, not offering anyone a cup of that scorched coffee, then Mike said: "Now that you're in the frame of mind for it, suppose the pair of us ride out to Flying E and bring in Eagleton."

Lew listened to this but seemed not greatly concerned. Mahoney, however, ripped out two swear words. "You're crazy if you think just two of you could arrest Cyrus Eagleton out at Flying E. Ayers, you're worth a thousand dollars dead. And you, Sheriff. . . ."

"Yeah, what about me? Have I got a price on my scalp, too?"

"Well, no, but Eagleton and Lefty are sort of off you for the stand you been takin' lately against Flying E. I wouldn't bet no money you'd ride out of that yard alive if you rode in with only one man at your side."

"Humph," growled Lew, "I've been stepping wide around Eagleton for long enough. I figure it's about time he learned to step wide around me for a while."

Lew stood up, picked up his ring of cell-block keys, and peremptorily jerked his head. Mahoney got up, walked ten feet away from the chair he'd been occupying, and out of the black night beyond the jailhouse's little grilled front window a Winchester roared.

Mike Ayers reacted instinctively to this. He threw himself sideways and downward, drew his six-gun, and rolled for a snap shot out that little window. Glass broke with a *crash* as Lew Burton also swung, dropped to one knee, and got off a shot.

This happened too fast, too entirely unexpectedly for either of those two men to catch the full significance until they'd hung there for ten seconds, waiting for another assassin's shot from out in the night. When this never came, they looked at one another, then over at Turk Mahoney. He was lying upon his back, both arms outflung, as dead as a dead-center .30-30 slug could make him.

Somewhere on across the road and beyond the store fronts a dog began to bark furiously. As Lew got up stiffly, holstered his gun, and bent to stare at Mahoney, Mike Ayers listened to that dog. The assassin, he was sure, had fled eastward where he'd undoubtedly had his horse tied. This was what had upset someone's watchdog.

"Deader'n a damned fence post," said Lew.

Mike gazed solemnly upon Mahoney. "They were probably waiting at the ranch for him to come back and report. He didn't come, so one of 'em rode over to Halfmoon, found no trace of me in the yard dead, rode on down here, saw the light in this office, got up to the window, heard enough, and killed him."

"About like that," agreed Lew. "My witness against Eagleton and Doolin, dog-gone it anyway."

"You've got another witness, Lew. His transcript or confession or whatever you call that thing, signed in his hand, and duly witnessed."

Lew's head jerked up as though he'd temporarily forgotten Mahoney's signed statement. "Sure," he said. "And whoever dry-gulched him thought he was keeping Turk from informing against the others. By golly, Ayers, this might work out after all."

Lew stepped to the door, opened it a crack, peered out, opened it wider, and stepped out into nighttime darkness. Alturas slumbered on. If that rash of fast gunshots had awakened anyone, he did not choose to step outside to investigate. The roadway's broad length was totally empty, not even a dog was visible on it from north to south.

Lew came out, half closed the door to minimize backgrounding light, cleared his throat, spat, and said: "I guess Mahoney was right. We'd better not ride out there just the pair of us. Eagleton will know as soon as whoever shot Turk gets back, that we know now what his part's been in this mess."

Mike stood there in pleasant nighttime coolness and shrugged. "That's up to you. If you want to, I'll go out there with you."

"Against those odds, and them all up by now and alert?"

"Lots of ways to skin a cat, Sheriff. Lots of ways."

Lew considered Ayers's expressionless face a second, screwed his eyes up sardonically, and said: "I'd like to see sixty. They tell me that's when life really begins."

Mike turned and smiled. Lew Burton could be droll, too. Mike's liking of the grizzled lawman increased. "Have it your way. I'll meet you here in the morning when you make up a posse."

Lew nodded, watched Ayers strike on out across the roadway toward the boarding house, and was turning to reënter his office when a man in slapping slippers came trotting along from northward. Lew stopped, squinted, then said: "Is that you, Amos? What the devil're you doin' abroad this time o' night?"

"I was just getting ready for bed, Lew. What was all that shooting about?"

Burton pushed open the office door so that Darren could see the corpse lying in there. Darren sucked back a sharp breath.

"Turk. That's Turk Mahoney. Is he dead?"

"As dead as a man can get from a Winchester slug through his heart from the back, Amos."

Darren swung. "You, Lew?"

"Nope. Someone shot from out here through my little office window. It was pretty neat, Amos. Neither Ayers nor I dared jump out after him, so he got away."

"Ayers was here with you?"

"Why don't you stop askin' so many questions and go on back to bed?"

"But who did it, Lew?"

"Who do you think would have reason to do it? I arrested Turk tonight up at Halfmoon in the hayloft waitin' to dry-gulch Ayers. Eagleton paid him to do that, so who'd be wanting him killed before he could talk too much, Amos?"

"But Lew, Eagleton's crew was all in town tonight. I saw 'em. So did John. So did most of. . . ."

"All of 'em, Amos?" asked Burton, and shook his head at the saloon man. "Not Turk Mahoney. But I know all about that anyway, so go on home, Amos. I'm tired."

Lew stepped in, blew out his table lamp, stepped back out, slammed the jailhouse door, barred it, and started past.

Amos Darren said: "Lew, you're not going to leave Turk lying in there like that, are you?"

Burton turned, sighed, put a disgusted look upon the barman, and said: "Now what's wrong with leaving him like that, Amos? Confound it, he's dead. He's neither in pain nor hungry. And he sure as hell isn't going anywhere. Now, dog-gone it, go on home!"

Lew strode off, leaving Darren standing there in the silent night with a dead man lying just beyond the jailhouse door behind him. Ten feet farther along, after leaving the saloon man, Lew's thoughts turned to the morrow. He did not want to go after Cyrus Eagleton with a posse for the elemental reason that he knew Eagleton would put up a fight if he saw a crowd of armed horsemen coming, and yet, as he walked toward the boarding house, he could think of no other way of apprehending Eagleton unless he simply sat back and waited for the cowman to return to town.

In the end that's what he did, but inadvertently, not by design, because the following morning he'd no sooner had Turk Mahoney lugged down to the doctor's embalming shed than Ed Grosson came in to say confidentially that Cyrus Eagleton had withdrawn $10,000 in cash from his bank account the day before. Ed then proceeded to tell Lew something that interested him more. Eagleton had telegraphed a man named Mort Saltzer up in Cheyenne to bring two companions and come at once to Flying E.

To this last Lew said: "How do you know he wired Saltzer?"

"I read the copy of the wire, that's how," said Grosson.

"You mean that mangy telegraph clerk let you read a private wire?"

Grosson's face turned dark. "Now, you listen here," he said wrathfully. "This is no time for niceties. You know who Mort Saltzer is as well as I do. He's a two-gun man and a hired killer, and he comes almighty high. I don't want bank money used in some war Eagleton's gotten up with Ayers."

"And just how do you propose to stop him from doing it, Ed? Slap his face with a chattel mortgage or something?"

Grosson stood there glowering, was still glowering when Mike Ayers entered the jailhouse office freshly shaved and clothed. He nodded noncommittally at Grosson, took in Lew's irate expression, and said: "Ready to ride?"

Lew swung away from the banker. "You been down to see Buel?" he asked, knowing the answer to this even before Ayers inclined his head.

"He's doing fine. I told him about Mahoney. I also told him who it was that downed him from behind."

"What?" said Ed Grosson, speaking up suddenly. "You fellers know who shot Buel?"

Ayers put a quiet gaze upon the banker without answering. He studied big Ed Grosson from toes to poll and didn't say a word.

"We know," growled Lew. "Now go on over to the bank, Ed, and let us handle this."

"Eagleton? Lew, did Eagleton have anything to do with it?"

Before the lawman could answer, Mike Ayers spoke up, still gazing coolly at the banker. "What's your interest, mister?" he asked.

"My name's Grosson. I'm head of the bank across the road."

"All right," said Ayers in that same cool tone, "now I know your name. What I asked was what your interest is?"

Grosson, stung by Ayers's look and tone, colored. He considered the gunfighter for a moment as though he wished mightily to say something sharply back to him. But he didn't; he simply spun on his heel and left the office, each footfall striking hard down upon the yonder plank walk.

"Not very sociable cuss," murmured Ayers, then forgot the banker. "Where's the posse, Sheriff?"

Lew hung fire over his reluctant answer to this, and into this little intervening silence came the unmistakable beat of many ridden horses coming into Alturas from the northeast, all in a rushing body.

Ayers turned, stepped to the door, craned northward, remained motionless for a long second, then sighed and stepped back. "I reckon we won't need a posse," he told Lew. "That's Eagleton and his crew. They're heading this way and they're armed to the ears."

XIV

Lew took a sawed-off shotgun from his wall gun rack, stepped around Ayers, and into the doorway, his face craggy and his eyes drawn out narrowly.

"He made a mistake this time," he growled to Ayers. "A bad mistake."

Mike let Lew pass on out onto the plank walk in front of his office before he moved at all. It occurred to Mike that Eagleton knew the sheriff would arrest him. There was a slim possibility that Eagleton's assassin had not arrived at the jailhouse in time to hear Mahoney's confession, and, of course, if that had happened, then Eagleton would not yet know just how thorough Burton's knowledge of Eagleton's implication in two attempted murders was.

But Mike preferred the alternative to this, he preferred to accept the idea that Eagleton *did* know that he was now a wanted man, and had come riding into Alturas with his tough Texas crew for a fight. Mike preferred to act on this premise for the basic reason that, if he and Lew Burton were prepared for the worst, anything less than that would take care of itself. He did not approach the same doorway beyond which Lew was waiting with his riot gun. Instead, he passed across to the rifle rack, took down a carbine, checked it for loads, then went to the little broken window, stood off to one side, pushed back his hat, and rested the tip of his Winchester upon the sill. He had an excellent view of the roadway with its dazzling bright sun smash and its traffic. He saw that body of dusty horsemen rein indifferently through pedestrians and other riders, scattering both with an arrogant disdain, and slow when they were about 200 feet north of the jailhouse. They had seen Lew standing there under his jailhouse overhang with that double-barreled shotgun.

Eagleton was in the lead. Less than twenty feet behind him came Lefty Doolin. Behind Doolin ranged the other Flying E men, each with his belted six-gun and each with a booted carbine riding under the *rosadero* of every saddle. Mike watched them all, but that dull carbine snout, where it lay upon the window sill, tracked Lefty Doolin.

Eagleton drew rein out in the roadway, swung so that his horse was pointing head-on, and straightened up in the saddle. He put both hands atop his saddle horn and gazed across where Lew stood. Around him his tough Texans drew in close and also halted.

"I got a hunch," said Eagleton to Lew Burton, "that you'd like to arrest me, Sheriff. How about it?"

Mike could not see more of Lew than his profile, but he heard Lew's reply to that question well enough. "Not just like to, Eagleton, going to."

Eagleton shook his head gently, his eyes ranging along the jailhouse front as though searching for something or someone. "Naw, Sheriff, you don't want me for a prisoner. You got no charge that'd stick."

"Killing Mahoney won't save you, Eagleton."

The lank cowman's eyes dropped back to Lew's face. They were sardonic. "Is Mahoney dead?" he asked, then made an exaggerated head wag. "My, that's too bad, isn't it?"

"Yeah," growled Lew, "it's too bad. But I didn't

need him as a witness against you anyway, Eagleton, because I've got something just as good for my purpose."

"And what's your purpose, Sheriff?"

"Arrestin' you an' bringin' you to trial for assault with intent to kill an' for complicity in another attempted murder . . . the one you offered Mahoney a thousand dollars to commit. I want both you and Lefty Doolin."

Lew, watching Eagleton's face, saw now that Eagleton in fact had not known up to now whether or not Mahoney had talked. But now he *did* know; it showed in the way he kept staring down at Sheriff Burton. It also showed in what Eagleton said next.

"Sounds to me, Sheriff," he said from the saddle, "as though Mahoney talked himself to death."

This innuendo tickled Flying E's range boss. Doolin smiled, looked over at Eagleton in appreciation, then back down at Lew again. Eagleton spoke again.

"What is it you've got . . . another witness?"

"A witnessed confession by Mahoney of everything you've tried to do to get rid of Buel and Ayers, signed and sealed an' ready to be presented in court against you."

"I see," said the hawk-faced cowman, and briefly lapsed into thoughtful silence. Mike, watching closely now because he knew that, if trouble started, it would very shortly erupt, saw the rough, hard cast of Eagleton's features. There was no fear there; there was not even any uneasiness. Lew began to wonder about this. Eagleton's boldness in riding in to chouse Lew Burton had not been entirely bravado; he had something else to support his position. Lew was sure of that. He tried to deduce what this could be but didn't get far because Eagleton spoke out again.

"Sheriff," he said conversationally, completely un-mindful that northward a discreet distance the roadway and both plank walks were filled by curious onlooking townspeople, that traffic was nearly at a standstill, and that every one of those viewing spectators saw in Flying E's heavily armed presence the prelude to bad trouble. "Sheriff, let's talk this out. You're tryin' to tie me to attempted murders."

"And one completed one . . . Mahoney."

"All right, two attempted ones and one completed one," agreed Eagleton in the same quiet, inflection-less tone. "And you aim to arrest me."

"I *am* arresting you, Eagleton."

"Naw, I don't think so. And I'll tell you why, Burton." Eagleton lifted his shoulders, twisted in the saddle, and looked over the heads of his riders to the *Clarion's* office. "Arnold ought to be here," he said without straightening back around. "He'd like to take all this down for use in his damned little rag."

Mike watched the cowman twist back to put his arrogant gaze down on Lew Burton. Something stirred in Mike. He began to have a premonition about Eagleton's boldness.

"Where is Arnold, Sheriff?"

Lew said nothing. Mike strained closer to the wall to catch sight of Burton's face. He thought the sheriff must also be beginning to understand this game Eagleton was playing.

"You don't know, do you, Sheriff? I'll tell you where Arnold is. Hidden in a cave in the Horseshoe Hills, and he's going to stay there until I'm finished with Ayers and this stinkin' little town." Eagleton paused, lifted his lips in a thin smile at Lew, and concluded with: "An' Sheriff, if you try to lock me up, you'll probably get killed in the attempt. But if you don't an' if I get locked up . . . John Arnold dies!"

Lew stood there without moving. Mike could still not make out his expression but he had no trouble interpreting the fighting-mad and wrathful way Lew was standing, the way he was glaring out at Cyrus Eagleton.

For sixty seconds no one said anything. Eagleton and Burton kept up that uncompromising exchange of stares. Doolin and the other Flying E men sat like stone, waiting. Northward along the plank walks men began to thin out, to head for recessed doorways or to step inside. That terrible silence was the kind that usually preceded a volley of gunfire.

Eagleton lifted his reins, turned his horse, and hung there for a second to see what Burton would do. When Lew did nothing at all, Eagleton's scorning smile came up again. He said quietly to his men— "Come on, let's go."—and walked his horse back northward up the bitter yellow roadway through the hush and the dry-eyed, hooded stares of all those motionless townspeople.

Mike withdrew the Winchester, leaned it aside, and went out to Lew. There, the pair of them stood in sweaty shade watching Flying E depart from the town. While he was still watching those riders, Mike said: "He was pretty busy last night, and, if I hadn't been in such a hurry to get over here this morning, I'd have gone by to see Evelyn, and we'd have known what else he did last night."

"I never sold him short," mumbled Lew, easing back to place both shoulders against the front of his jailhouse. "But I sure never anticipated this. It's a wonder to me that he didn't call you out. He must have known you were in there."

"He wouldn't do that, Sheriff. Eagleton's no coward, I'm convinced of that, but he wouldn't take that long a chance when he doesn't have to. He kills from ambush, or he hires it done. He wouldn't call me out. He doesn't have to."

"Yeah," muttered Lew, seeing two big shapes detach themselves from those northward spectators and start down toward him with thrusting strides. "Here comes the belly-achin' committee . . . Grosson an' Darren. Let's go inside."

Mike followed Lew into the office. With his back to Mike as he put up the shotgun, Lew said: "Did you ever hear of a man named Mort Saltzer?"

Mike eased down on the cane-bottomed chair, nodding his head. "Two-gun man," he said with no show of interest. "Hangs out at the Drover's Club up in Cheyenne. What about him?"

Lew turned, walked to his desk, and sat down before he answered. "Yesterday Eagleton wired him to come to Alturas and fetch along a couple of friends."

Mike's face did not alter expression but his eyes swung, and they now showed hard interest. "Well, like I just said outside, Lew, Eagleton hires his killings done."

"Saltzer's got one hell of a reputation, boy."

"So I've heard."

These two might have said more on the subject of Eagleton's hired two-gun man, but they didn't get a chance. Grosson and Amos Darren walked in, both puffing from exertion in that outside blistering heat, and both looked anguished. Grosson, the better dressed of the two, took out a handkerchief and mopped his face with it. Darren stepped past to the drinking water, took up a dipper full, and noisily swallowed.

Grosson said: "Lew, why did you let him ride out of town like that? You had a shotgun."

Mike looked quickly at Grosson, his gaze turning milky with indignation. "Mister," he said evenly, "just what do you want from the sheriff? If you're so damned dumb you don't know yet that even a riot gun's no match for nearly a half dozen six-guns, then you better get out of here and go back to compounding your lousy interest."

This knife-edged denunciation turned Amos Darren stiff over where he was holding the dipper. He looked straight at Mike Ayers and there was a lot of respect in Darren's heavy face. As a saloon man he'd heard most of the gunfighting legends about Ayers and he did not now like the idea of being in the same room with Ayers when he was as obviously annoyed as he now was.

Grosson knew some of those legends so he, too, stood there looking and saying nothing, but the irritation at Lew Burton did not depart from his features.

It was Lew who broke this awkward moment. He said mildly: "There's something you two don't know, Ed. I didn't have any alternative and it had nothing to do with Eagleton's guns."

Lew arose, ambled over to his stove, went to work there in silence for a few moments, putting coffee on to boil, then he turned, looked at Grosson, and said in the same mild tone: "Have either of you seen John Arnold this morning?" When neither Darren nor Grosson answered this, Lew nodded at Mike Ayers. "Tell them."

"Eagleton kidnapped Arnold some time last night. He's holding him hostage." Mike watched those two faces turn slack, turn incredulous. He made a bleak grin at Ed Grosson. "Now, tell me, Mister Banker, do you still think we should've pushed Flying E into a gunfight?"

Grosson didn't answer. Over by the water bucket Amos Darren turned, very carefully hung the dipper back upon its nail, very slowly turned back facing Mike, and leaned upon the office wall, his expression stunned, his attitude speechless.

"Let me say this," said Ayers to that pair of townsmen. "The worst kind of judgment is the kind you two just made . . . a snap judgment of your sheriff. If you'd come bustin' in here at me like that, I'd have taken off that damned badge and handed it to you. Then you could figure out what to do."

Grosson went to a chair and sank down. "But, hell," he weakly said, "we didn't know."

Mike shook his head. "Your kind never does, but that doesn't seem to keep you from mouthing off."

Lew crossed to his desk, rummaged for a cigar, found one, and lit it. He could've eased the discomfort of Grosson and Darren, but he didn't; instead, he thoughtfully smoked, timed his coffee, and waited out a long moment of silence before Grosson looked over at him.

"What are you going to do, Lew?"

"Try to save John naturally."

"And Eagleton . . . ?"

"He can wait. Right now John's more important."

Grosson nodded agreement with this. He pushed heavily up out of the chair, looked at Darren, and jerked his head. The two of them got almost to the door before Lew spoke again.

"Don't breathe a word of this to anyone," he cautioned. "I don't want angry townsmen formin' up into lynch mobs and rushin' out to fight Flying E."

Darren said—"Sure not, Lew."—and preceded the banker out of the office.

When they were alone again, Mike raised an eyebrow at Lew. "He asked a good question, Sheriff, just what *are* you going to do?"

Lew emitted a great cloud of smoke. "I was goin' to ask you for help," he said, bent, picked up a little circlet of metal from among the disarray atop his desk, and tossed it over. "You're deputized. Pin it on and let's do some planning."

XV

Evelyn was there when Mike Ayers and Sheriff Burton strolled solemnly up to the Arnold front porch. It was near ten o'clock and she told them Smoky was sleeping, that he'd eaten a big breakfast, and had drunk two cups of coffee.

Ayers and Burton exchanged a look, then Lew asked Evelyn where her father was. "Arose early this morning," she answered calmly, "and went down to the office, I presume. At least he was gone when I got up."

Ayers and Burton exchanged another look. Neither of them said a thing for a moment, then Mike asked if they could see Smoky for a short visit. Evelyn didn't like the idea of awakening Buel, but she acquiesced and led them inside. She turned just outside Smoky's door and asked if Lew wanted to see her father about anything in particular. Sheriff Burton shook his head; he had already come to the conclusion that for now, at least, he would not tell Evelyn about her father's abduction. Mike sensed this attitude and went along with it. When Evelyn volunteered to bring coffee for them, Mike said he'd help her in the kitchen. She and Mike walked away, leaving Lew a clear field with Smoky Buel.

When they were together in the big, airy kitchen, Evelyn said: "I'm glad you didn't get ambushed up at Halfmoon."

Mike squinted over at her. "How did you know an ambush was planned?"

"Uncle Lew and my father discussed it. Dad told me."

Mike nodded. It didn't matter, really, that she knew; they were both on the same side.

He watched her work; she was smooth in her movements, and efficient. Once, as she passed close, he felt an urge to touch her, to reach out and keep her from moving on. He didn't, and he was surprised at himself for entertaining the notion. He was not a woman's man, never had been, in fact, although he'd known his share of women. He'd seldom seen any that caught his attention, certainly never one that tugged at him against his will as this one did. Evelyn turned and smiled at him. Against his will? He shook his head over that.

"Is something the matter?" she asked, seeing that faint head shake.

"You," he said, holding her gaze. "Just you, ma'am."

Suddenly there was that same electric atmosphere there in the kitchen with them. Evelyn's little smile turned uncertain, turned self-conscious, but she did not drop her eyes from his face. Words formed on her lips; he saw them lying there, but she did not utter them. Instead, she swung away from him and put cups on a tray, put a cream pitcher and a sugar bowl on it, and said, still with her back to him: "Do you plan to stay in Washoe County?"

He leaned upon the wall with his dusty hat in one hand. "Wild horses couldn't drag me away," he said, his voice soft toward her, his double meaning clear enough so that, over by the stove, she ceased moving altogether, but still did not turn to face him.

"Halfmoon is a fine ranch," she murmured. "I

used to ride up there quite a lot when your uncle was alive. It's beautiful in the springtime."

Now she turned. He saw the deep sweep of a long breath lift her breasts. She looked straight at him.

"When this is all over, I'd like to ride up there again."

"I'll be unhappy if you don't, Miss Evelyn. And you could show me the range. So far I haven't had a chance to cover very much of it."

"I'd be glad to."

He stood admiring her and letting an awkwardness come between them. He sought for words to break the silence but couldn't find any appropriate ones, and was relieved when she said: "Smoky has told me a lot about you."

"Well," he said a little dryly, "don't believe all of it."

"But I do believe him. He doesn't think there's ever been a man like you."

"You see," he said, coloring. "You know that's not so. And some of those things he's undoubtedly told you . . . I didn't go looking for them."

"I believe that," she said. "Tell me one thing. If you settle down to operating Halfmoon, do you mean to work at it? I mean, will you be content at ranching after all the exciting things you've done?"

Her eyes were warm to him; they saw deeply inside him and he felt a trifle uncomfortable because of that. "I aim to cow ranch for the rest of my days. What's gone before is behind me, Miss Evelyn. A man gets to an age, after a while, when he doesn't crave excitement. He craves something else."

"Oh . . . ?"

"A home, a good ranch."

"Yes?"

Mike smiled over at her. "A . . . well . . . a good, normal life. You know what I mean."

"I'm not sure. Tell me."

His smile got strained. He said: "I'm not very good at this kind of talk." He took a deep breath. "A wife an' kids and all that goes with them."

He waited, expecting something to happen, something he was not sure of at all. When nothing happened at all and Evelyn only said—"Of course."—he felt as though he'd jumped into space and had been left hanging there.

"Of course. You wouldn't want to live up there all alone like your Uncle Pete did."

She poured the coffee, put the pot aside, brushed back a heavy auburn curl from her cheek, and started to lift the tray. In two big strides he was at her side, reaching. She turned, half stepping clear so he could take the tray, but somehow Mike was never afterward clear about how, he did not touch the tray, he touched her, caught her at the waist with both hands, turned her, and drew her to him.

She did not offer resistance, but she was stiff in his arms and her heavy lips lay parted in surprise. She looked up at him, her eyes darker than usual.

This strange moment lasted for several seconds before his head dropped; he sought her mouth and she strained upward to meet his lowering lips.

It was a tender kiss.

She put both palms against him and pushed, not hard but enough to loosen his hold. He released her and stood there, feeling awkward, feeling embarrassed and a little ashamed.

She brushed at that heavy red-gold curl again, half swung away, and reached for the tray as though nothing had happened between them. He considered this a rebuff and wished himself miles away.

But she did not pick up the tray, after all. She simply stood there, gazing down at it for a while before she turned her face to him, and smiled.

"Would you like to try that again," she asked gently, "when I'm expecting it?"

He tried to match her smile with a grin of his own, but it was not a total success, so he reached for her with his expression solemn, his heart pounding loudly enough for them both to hear.

This time she came to him without stiffness. She put both hands against him to protect herself, leaned up onto her toes, and met his mouth with tenderness, with a sweet fragrance that threw him off balance. Instead of being gentle as before, he burned her with his hunger and his want. She met his fire with a sudden, unexpected fire of her own that afterward left them both weak and a little breathless.

They stood like that, holding one another, until somewhere down the hall a man's spurred boots came solidly toward them. They sprang apart, she scarlet, he fumbling with the laden tray.

Lew Burton pushed on into the kitchen, started to say something, stopped frozen, staring at those two flaming faces with his jaw hanging slackly, then stepped back as Mike shouldered past him without a glance or a word, followed by Evelyn. Lew let them get almost to the door of Buel's room before he remembered himself, moved away from the kitchen door, and went along after them.

Smoky was sitting up in bed when Mike entered with Evelyn. He quirked a grin at Ayers, saying: "Burton thought you two was out there long enough to grow the coffee beans an' went after you." He'd no sooner finished saying this than Lew, also, came into the room. Smoky's shrewd eyes caught something here but he could not define it, nor did he try very long because Mike handed him a full cup of coffee that called upon all his powers of balance to keep from spilling.

An awkward little period of time passed when none of them had anything to say. Lew blew on his coffee, sipped it with the critical skepticism of a professional coffee maker, and by then he'd had sufficient time to erase entirely all the embarrassment and astonishment from his face, so he sat there looking blandly at his coffee as expressionless as a graven image, but busy with his private thoughts until Smoky spoke to Mike.

"If you fellers are goin' after that Doolin feller, I'd like to ride along in a buggy."

"You," said Mike severely, "will ride this bed, and you won't ride it out of this room. What's the doctor say about your side?"

"Healing well enough. Mike, how could a little buggy ride hurt?"

Ayers studied his pardner's face and saw at once that Lew had told Smoky about Evelyn's father. The strained, veiled look of fierce hostility was there. He said, gazing deeply into Buel's eyes: "Never mind. What's got to be done, Sheriff Burton and I'll take care of." Mike remembered something, rummaged in a shirt pocket, brought forth his little circlet, and palmed it for Buel to see. "I'm also the law hereabouts now," he said, beginning a slow smile. "And my first order is that you stay right here where you are."

"There are a half dozen of 'em," growled Buel. "Not to mention Mort Saltzer."

Evelyn, in the act of sipping coffee, looked sharply at Mike, then on over to Lew Burton. "Saltzer," she said quickly. "That two-gun man who's had those things written about him in the Cheyenne newspapers?"

Mike glared at Smoky. Lew Burton put that bland look over at Evelyn. "Just talk," he said reassuringly. "Just a rumor, Evvie. He's probably not comin' down to Alturas at all."

"Uncle Lew," the beautiful girl said in that quiet, tough way she had of speaking that was half warning, half accusation.

Burton lifted both shoulders and let them fall. "All right. Ed Grosson said Eagleton sent for Saltzer, said he saw a copy of the telegram. But Evvie. . . ."

"Uncle Lew, from what I've read, that man is nothing but a professional killer." Evelyn set her cup back on the tray. It made a little *clatter* there that sounded extremely loud in the otherwise stillness. She looked from Lew to Mike, her expression showing quick concern.

"*Aw*, now," said Lew, still trying to placate her. "Don't fret, Evvie. If he shows up . . . and I'm not convinced that he will . . . we'll be ready for him. You know what they say about the forewarned bein' forearmed . . . or something like that."

Smoky hid himself by slowly drinking his cup dry and flitting his glance from one of those faces to the others. When Mike turned his accusing glance away, Smoky lowered the cup, put it aside, and ran one hand scratchily over his unshaven jowl.

It was Mike who finally arose, took up his hat, and motioned his head toward the sheriff and the door. He hesitated a moment in front of Evelyn, put out a hand, and, when she lay her fingers on his palm, he closed his hand tightly around them. Neither of them spoke. He let go of her fingers, stepped past to the door, and waited until Sheriff Burton moved on around him into the yonder hall.

"You remember what I said," he told Smoky. "If Evvie tells me you got out of that bed, I'll come back and stove in the other side of your rib box."

Mike was moving off when Smoky said: "Mike? I'm sorry."

"Forget it. You and I've met our share of Mort Saltzers before."

"Yeah, but I won't be with you this time."

"Lew Burton will. Next to you I'd take him any day."

Evelyn got up, walked over where Mike stood in the doorway, halted, and stood there. Those two exchanged a long look without speaking. Mike raised a hand, brushed fingers across her smooth cheek, let the hand drop, and swung out of the room. Evelyn did not follow after him, and back in his bed Smoky Buel sat there with his mouth hanging open and both eyes wide and glassy. He'd never before seen Mike Ayers with that look on his face; he'd never before seen him touch a woman as he'd touched Evelyn Arnold.

For a long time after they'd both heard that front door close, neither Smoky nor Evelyn said a thing. She went back, gravely gathered up the cups, put them upon the tray, stood for a while gazing downward, then she lifted wet-shiny eyes to Smoky and said very softly: "Nothing can happen to him, Smoky. If it does, I don't know what I'll do."

Smoky Buel was completely at a loss, but he struggled, he fought hard to find something appropriate to say, and it was everlastingly to his credit that he found the right words.

"Nothing will, Miss Evelyn. Not when he's got as fine a reason as you are, to come back here."

"Smoky . . . ?"

"Yes'm?"

"Why hasn't he ever married?"

Smoky had to struggle again. "Well, he just never has. Sometimes folks just don't. It's not real unusual, ma'am."

"Was there a girl, sometime, who . . . hurt him?"

"No ma'am." Smoky pondered, then said: "But I can tell you this, because I know him that well . . . there sure is one now."

XVI

As they were walking back toward Main Street, Lew Burton said: "I told Smoky the whole story."

"I know you did. I saw it in his face."

"He shouldn't have let it slip about Saltzer."

"It could've been worse," said Mike. "He could've let it slip about her pa. Tell me, Sheriff, how did Eagleton manage that without Evelyn knowing?"

"That wouldn't have been hard. John putters around in his garden evenings. Sometimes, too, he sits out on his porch for an hour or two after supper. No, slipping up and getting him without Evelyn knowing about it wouldn't have been hard. But I'll tell you one thing. Flying E sure was busy last night."

Lew looked over at Mike's thoughtful profile as they paced along; it was grave and resolute, but it was also softly tender. Lew cleared his throat and groped for some way to mention Evelyn. He didn't complete this effort, for Ayers shot him a knowing look.

"How'd she come to call you Uncle Lew?" he asked.

"Her mother died young. I sort of helped her grow up, but we're not related. She's a fine girl, Mike, a fine girl. To know just how good she really is a man'd have to know her a long time."

"I'd like to," murmured Mike, then picked up his gait, forcing Lew to hasten to keep up, and in this manner closing off all further discussion of Evelyn Arnold. As they swept around onto Main Street, Mike said: "Where will they be holding Arnold?"

Lew puffed along, wagging his head. "Never heard of any caves in the Horseshoe Hills, so I wouldn't know. Say, what's the blasted hurry?"

Mike slowed. Across from them the livery barn hostler was standing in his shaded doorway, chewing a straw and looking out over the town. Directly opposite him was Darren's Bar with several drowsing saddle animals tied to its rack. At the bank two sturdy cattlemen emerged to stand briefly together talking, and down by the local pool hall a number more cow ponies were tied outside.

"Seems like quite a number of cowmen in town," said Mike, looking along that hot, dusty roadway. "There hasn't been this many since I've been here, Lew."

Burton ran an appraising glance north and south. When he recognized that this was so, he dourly grunted. "One thing you can say for cattlemen. When there's trouble, they can scent it ten miles off. They don't like to miss any excitement."

"In that case," Mike said thoughtfully, "let's give 'em a chance to share in it."

"Huh? How?"

"There's a lot of 'em, Lew."

"You already pointed that out."

"And the Horseshoe Hill range is pretty large."

"So."

"So, let's round up fifty or so of them, deputize 'em, ride up there, and spread 'em out in a surround that's a couple of miles square, then have them ride slowly inward from all sides of Flying E."

Burton listened to this idea with a frown, and

doubtfully said: "You heard Eagleton. He'd kill Arnold."

"I doubt it very much, Lew. Arnold's the only assurance he's got you won't pull him apart. Furthermore, Eagleton may be tough an' he may be no coward, but I studied him close in front of the jailhouse and I'll tell you this about him . . . he's no fool. He's not going to buck fifty cowmen with his six Texans. Not if he sees he can't possibly win."

"I've never known Cyrus Eagleton to back down in his life," said Lew, still doubtful about all this. "And we've got to think of John Arnold."

"I am thinking about Arnold, Lew. But I'm also thinking of something else. You can't do business with men like Eagleton unless you're willing to do it on their terms, and, believe me, if you hesitate now, you're lost. Eagleton'll keep Arnold and he'll ride roughshod over your whole county."

It was a tough decision for Lew Burton. If Ayers's idea failed, John Arnold would be killed. On the other hand, what Mike had said was true enough and Lew recognized this, too. He'd already given Eagleton more rope than he should have.

"All right. Let's go recruit our posse and be on our way."

But Mike shook his head. "You recruit 'em," he said. "I'll get our horses from the livery barn and meet you there. These cowmen not only don't know me, they've probably heard enough adverse rumors to hang back a little if they think I'm involved." Mike had yet another reason for not going with Lew, but he did not mention it.

Lew squinted up at the sun, estimated the number of daylight hours left, nodded without looking at Ayers, and hiked off bound for Darren's Bar.

Mike let him go, watched until Lew swung in up at Amos Darren's place, then turned and walked as far as the telegraph office. There he remained for some little time before emerging and hastening across to the livery barn. The hostler jerked to life as Mike called sharply for his and the lawman's horses.

A little later men began drifting northward along Main Street, some leisurely walking beside their saddled animals, others riding. The number of these cowboys and cowmen steadily increased until, a half hour later, the entire town became aware that something unusual was in progress. Merchants stood in their doorways, looking over at the steadily augmenting crowd of horsemen. Even Ed Grosson, apprised by one of his clerks that a big posse was being gotten up, came out as far as the bank's street side entrance and stood there, peering through hard yellow sun smash at the increasing body of horsemen.

Mike Ayers sat his horse just inside the barn's shady doorway. He had Lew's mount in hand. His face was pensively unreadable and he remained a little apart from those men farther out, who were joking back and forth in the manner of rough range riders, unconcerned that within another hour or two they might be facing hostile guns.

Mike made a critical inspection of the men Lew had sent to the livery barn. He did not expect to find them any different than they were, although, because the fraternity of cattlemen and cowboys, coming as each did from an identical environment, never was different.

These were hard men but fair; they could fight and they would fight. They were rough, sturdy, courageous men with very elemental beliefs in right and wrong, and very elemental beliefs in how wrong should be punished. They would do, Mike thought. They would do perfectly for what he had in mind.

When Lew finally came across the road, he had with him three grizzled older men. Those three had that unmistakable air of authority that went with successful owners of big cow outfits. Mike sat back in shadows, watching Lew and those men; they halted out a way, talked intently together for a few minutes, then abruptly broke up, each cowman heading for some particular segment of that big crowd of riders. Lew spied Ayers back inside the barn and walked swiftly to him. Mike tossed Lew his reins and the sheriff stepped up over leather.

"It better work," he said. "I told 'em how we wanted this done . . . a big surround a couple miles out in all directions around Flying E, which they are to close slowly, drivin' any riders they meet out there into Flying E's yard as they close the circle." Lew adjusted his reins, settled deeper into his saddle, looked over at Mike, and said: "As for the shootin' . . . they're not to do a thing until you an' I give 'em the word."

Mike nodded approval. He said: "They won't need us, is that it?" He'd seen something in Lew's expression to inspire this question.

Lew looked around. "You got a habit of readin' my mind, Mike. I'm not sure whether I like that or not."

Ayers sat there nearly smiling at the craggy old lawman. "I guess, Lew," he drawled, "in some ways you and I are alike."

"What's that mean?"

"Well, Eagleton has made you look bad a few times. No man likes having that done to him, and usually he doesn't forget it. I'd say about now you're thinking of sort of evening that score up by riding into Flying E's yard and calling Eagleton in front of his crew. Right, Lew?"

"Dog-gone you," growled the sheriff, shook out his reins, and added: "Come on. If I'm doing something foolish, you don't have to go all the way with me. Yes, you're right. I want to make Eagleton eat crow in front of others just once, like he's done it to me."

As soon as Lew emerged from the dark livery barn with Mike Ayers, all that outside murmuring stopped. Men's eyes rose to those two, some turning wary, some turning interested, but all committed and therefore resolute. Lew did not speak; he simply flagged forward with an upflung arm and kept on riding.

Ed Grosson, over in the bank's doorway, darkly scowled, and the livery barn hostler broadly smiled. This was to a great extent symbolic of the mixed attitude of everyone who watched that big body of riders walk northward out of Alturas. The merchants, by now realizing their sheriff had no alternative to his present course, were still glum about what must now follow, while those like the hostler, with no private axes to grind, were delighted at the prospect of excitement in this dull, monotonous time of year. These people, too, sensitive to Flying E's long and arrogant reign, derived pleasure from the prospect of Cyrus Eagleton's humbling.

Among the posse men no such abstract factors entered the minds of most of those horsemen at all. They knew Flying E as well as they knew any other local outfit, but that was not, in their sight, the issue at hand. Eagleton had violated the law that served all of them and, whether he was one of them or not, did not now enter into it. Nevada was a raw land; the only safety for its people lay in support of their common beliefs, the common law. They rode now, riding to uphold that common law.

Of course, among the cowmen, there was some knowledge of Eagleton's arrogance, but mostly these were not owners, they were the riders who worked for the owners, therefore, being simple, forthright men, they viewed Eagleton' transgressions in a simple forthright manner.

Mike, seeing all those bronzed faces behind him as he paced along beside Sheriff Burton, did not believe Eagleton would resist; he thought Eagleton would fully understand what would follow if he did resist, because Flying E's owner was also a cowman; he knew how others of his kind thought and acted.

But uncertainty lingered, too, in Mike's mind, for no man could ever predict the course of other men with total accuracy. Take Lew. He understood perfectly how Lew felt, and yet he had reservations concerning the wisdom of riding into Eagleton's yard, just the pair of them, and attempting to lay down the law. He thought it would be far wiser to catch Eagleton out on the range, or even await him in Alturas for the showdown. But he did not say a word about any of this to Lew, and he would, reservations notwithstanding, ride into the Flying E yard with the sheriff.

For a full two miles that large party of men rode along in a leisurely manner with gray dust jerking to life underfoot, with the bitter sunlight across their shoulders and backs, and with casual conversation passing back and forth. Then they arrived at the fork in the easterly trail, and here they halted, while

Lew swung to face them and make a wide, circling movement with one upraised arm.

Only two men had questions. One of these asked what course to follow if they were fired upon before they got around Flying E. Lew fixed that cowboy with a flinty stare and said nothing. Several men made quiet chuckles and one older cowboy said: "Maybe, if you just close your eyes, they might not see you an' quit firing." This brought a splash of embarrassed color to the questioner's face and he subsided.

The second cowboy had a better inquiry. He wanted to know what course they should follow if a fight erupted in Flying E's yard.

"Fight back," snapped Lew. "And fight hard." Then he paused, held up a hand for absolute silence, looked out over those assembled, rough faces, and spoke again in a quieter way. "There's one thing I didn't tell any of you back in town because I didn't want the townsmen to hear this and get all worked up. Flying E has John Arnold, the *Clarion's* publisher, hostage. Eagleton said they're holding John in some cave in the hills, but I think they've got him on the ranch. Now, boys . . . be careful. If trouble starts, try to find out where Arnold is an' get to him before they shoot him. Mike Ayers here beside me doesn't think they'll kill him, and I sure hope he's right, but all the same . . . let's try and liberate him before that idea's put to the test."

Those range men sat there entirely silent, gazing ahead at the sheriff. When none of them spoke forth, an old cowman rumbled at Lew: "All right, let's quit wastin' time. We know what we're supposed to do."

Lew nodded at this man. "Sure, Charley," he said. "Ayers and I are going to ride on into the ranch yard and give Eagleton his chance to quit. We'll give you a half hour to get into place in the surround and start closin' in." Lew nodded again, this time with finality. "Good luck, boys."

Someone called softly: "Good luck to you, Sheriff. I got a feelin' you're goin' to need it a heap more'n we are."

Lew and Mike sat there as the crowd broke up, riders angling off in different directions, some of them loping apart from the others, but most of them traveling in little groups.

That angry, burning sun was an evil force throughout all this. It glittered off tiny mica particles in the rising dust, made the day evil and bitter, and turned men's thoughts to harsh things.

XVII

Riding slowly and close together, Lew and his new deputy came within sight of Flying E's functional, weathered buildings. North and west lay the Horseshoe Hills, but elsewhere roundabout lay the flat, sere plains of summertime Nevada.

The ranch seemed deserted, which gave Mike a bad moment. If, after all their preparations, Eagleton was not there with his crew, he and the sheriff would have to plan anew.

Evidently Lew had been thinking along these same lines for, when he spoke, his voice was soft with relief. "Yonder's a man," he said. "Passin' between the main house and the barn."

Mike picked up this moving shape, and evidently at the same time that man sighted the approaching riders because he abruptly stopped, staring against the shimmering distance straight out.

"He'll pass the word," muttered Mike, waiting for that cowboy to move.

He did. He turned, started for the bunkhouse, then, as though struck by another idea, altered his course quickly, making for Eagleton's residence on across the yard.

Neither Lew nor Mike had anything more to say. They were close to the yard now, close enough to see drowsing horses in the corrals and saddles atop the corral's uppermost stringer. Mike let Lew make the decision where they would halt, and Lew seemed to have already made up his mind about this.

They passed quietly into Flying E's yard surrounded by an endless, evil silence that appeared to compound the burning brightness of that fierce overhead sun. Heat waves danced across the plain and the faded overhead sky was raggedly pale at its outermost edges.

They were not yet past the barn when a man stepped loosely out upon the bunkhouse porch, looked north, stiffened long enough to recognize the oncoming riders, then whipped around and jumped back out of sight inside.

"That'll awaken 'em," stated Lew, keeping his eyes upon the bunkhouse. "It'll be like kickin' a hornets' nest."

Mike put his whole attention upon that bunkhouse and made no comment. He anticipated bad trouble now; it was like a pungent scent in the hot, still air. His every nerve was alive and receptive to this charged atmosphere. Things that ordinarily were hazily visible in heat blast like this were suddenly acutely clear in every detail to him. Eagleton's crew was in the bunkhouse, of that he was convinced, and very shortly now Eagleton himself would step out across the way. He looked from beneath his broad hat brim over at Lew. The sheriff was rocking along atop his horse with no appearance of anxiety at all, but up around the eyes Lew was different. It was hard to describe that difference but it was there, a narrowed, cautious watchfulness. A kind of unrelenting savagery that one fast move, one fierce word would trigger into blazing violence.

That man who had initially seen them riding in came forth from Eagleton's house, paused upon the porch to squint outward, shuffled his feet a little as though wondering whether to leave or stay, and in the end he struck out around the house to his left, disappeared around a corner, and was entirely lost to Mike's view.

"Sent him back to the bunkhouse by a round-about way," he muttered to Lew, "so we'll have guns behind us."

"He should've gone with him, because this way he's in front of us, and, if hell busts loose, he's sure to stop the first one."

But Lew's surmise proved incorrect, for as the pair of them reined down to a halt within ten feet of Eagleton's front verandah, the door opened and two men, not one, stepped out, Cyrus Eagleton and Lefty Doolin. Both those lank, sturdy men were iron-faced, both were armed, and neither one of them said a word as Lew put both his hands atop the saddle horn and leaned a little, gazing down at them where verandah shade gloomily softened the antagonism in their eyes.

"I've come for you two," said Lew. "I also want the man who assassinated Mahoney, whoever he is, and on general principles I'll take in the rest of your hands, too."

Eagleton lifted his gaze off Burton and put it upon Mike Ayers. His lips turned downward in a scornful expression. "Gunfighter," he said softly. "The famous Mike Ayers . . . gunfighter." He said no more for as long as it took him to range that contemptuous glance up and down Mike from boots to hat. "You look pretty confident, sittin' up there, Ayers. How confident would you feel if you knew you'd be dead in a couple more days?"

Mike, moving with exaggerated slowness so as

not to trigger the tightness in those two armed men across the porch from him, reached up, took a slip of yellow paper from his shirt pocket, and flicked it outward. The paper settled down a few feet in front of Eagleton.

Mike said: "Read it."

Neither Eagleton nor Doolin more than glanced down where the paper lay for a long time, but in each of their faces curiosity showed plainly enough.

"Go ahead," said Ayers. "No one's going to open up on you. Read it."

Eagleton still did not remove his glance from Mike, but he said: "Pick it up, Lefty."

Doolin did. He scooped the paper up with one hand, his other hand within inches of the saw handle of that holstered six-gun on his hip. He straightened back up and thrust the paper toward Eagleton, who took it. Now it was Doolin who kept watch while his employer unfolded the paper and studied it. As he was doing this, Mike spoke again.

"One thing about telegrams, Eagleton, they don't care whose name is at the bottom of 'em. I don't suppose, if I'd had to write Saltzer and sign your name, he'd have believed it had come from you. But with telegrams all the words are printed, so all I did was wire him a hundred dollars for his trouble, tell him you didn't need him after all, and put your name at the bottom of the thing."

Eagleton looked up. He clenched that slip of paper in his fist, crumbling it unmercifully. Mike's eyes held to the angry cowman's face.

"So if that's what you meant when you said I'd be dead in a couple of days, forget it. Mort Saltzer's not coming."

Eagleton ripped out a curse and flung down the

copy of Mike's telegram. He stood there, balancing a decision in his mind and each of the four of them knew what that decision was, that it could, if he made the wrong decision, result in the gunfire death of every one of them.

Lew spoke into the charged hush surrounding the shaded porch: "You bit off more than you could chew, Eagleton. Don't be a damned fool and compound it by starting something now you can't possibly complete."

"Can't I?" exclaimed the angry cowman. "Burton, you old simpleton, there are guns trained on your back right this minute. Did you figure you'd ride in here and . . . ?"

"Shut up, Eagleton," said Lew sharply. "Shut up and listen to me." All the restrained animosity of years showed in Burton's face now; he was no longer the easy-going, tolerant man his friends knew him to be. He was ready and willing to fight, and he was yeasty with resentment against the taller, younger man in front of him.

"There were a dozen ways you could've tried for Halfmoon, and maybe gotten it. You could've bought it. You've got more than enough money for that. But no, you were a tough Texan. You scairt folks out, you didn't buy 'em out. You used guns to get what you wanted, so you shot Buel, or had him shot, by that man standing right there beside you. Then you tried to engineer Ayers's murder, too. But that one failed, so you shot the man you'd sent after Ayers to keep him from talkin'." Lew paused, rocked back in his saddle without removing either hand from the saddle horn, and looked coldly down at Eagleton. "No matter how big a man is, Eagleton, no matter how much money he's got . . . he's never bigger'n the law. Today you're goin' to find that out. Now I'm goin' to ask you to bring John Arnold up here on this porch, *pronto*, and unbuckle that gun belt you're wearin', because if you don't. . . ."

Lew didn't finish it. He just sat there, staring downward, letting Eagleton and Doolin supply their own imagined answers to their remaining alternative to surrender.

"Why, you old damned fool," snarled Eagleton in a tone so deeply contemptuous each word was slurred. "All I have to do is raise my hand and you'll be dead before you hit the ground."

"And you," said Mike Ayers to Eagleton, "wouldn't get that hand six inches into the air before your head would be busted wide open like a rotten melon."

Lefty Doolin, quiet up to now, began to squint out at those two horsemen, his expression turning skeptical, turning a little perplexed and troubled. "Are you plumb serious?" he asked the sheriff. "Ridin' in here just the pair of you an' actually thinkin' you'd ride out alive again, with Flyin' E prisoners? Sheriff, what you got up your sleeve?"

Lew ignored Doolin. He was watching Cyrus Eagleton. "What about it?" he said. "You goin' to take off that gun or go for big casino?"

Eagleton turned, cleared his throat, and contemptuously spat aside. He acted as though he might walk back into his house. He looked out at Lew with that monumental scorn twisting his face into an ugly grimace. It was Mike Ayers who broke up that despising expression. Mike eased slowly forward in his saddle, kicked loose his right leg, and began to dismount. As he did this, he said: "The law isn't a couple of men comin' for you, Eagleton. The law's

the combined conviction of all your neighbors."
Mike stood easy with the yellow sunlight burning
against him at the side of his horse. He was holding
one split rein in his left hand. His right hand was
hanging almost straight down, but with a very
slight crook in it at the elbow. No sane, sober man,
seeing that stance, could have misunderstood it. Ayers was just about through talking. He was ready to
fight. But he went on speaking in the same quiet,
even tone as though nothing more than this conversation engaged his interest.

"You're not going up against just the sheriff and
me. You're buckin' all of Washoe County, all the Territory of Nevada, all of the people of this country,
and no man's big enough, no matter what he thinks
of himself, to take on odds like that. No man alive.
Not you or any other man, Eagleton. For myself I
hope you go for that gun. You too, Doolin. I owe you
somethin' for shootin' my pardner. I've been fightin'
your kind since I was eighteen years old. That's how
I got my reputation. But this time I aim to see legal
justice done instead of six-gun justice. So spit or
close the window . . . as Lew said, go for big casino
or take off those guns. Right damned now!"

For the length of a long, indrawn breath no one
said anything or moved or even shifted their eyes.
For Eagleton and Doolin this was it; each of them
recognized it, too, and each of them was cold and
calculatingly thoughtful. Burton was still up there
atop his horse, an easy target, but Ayers, standing at
an angle so that his own animal could, if he stepped
quickly enough, become a shield, was something
else again.

The advantage that Eagleton had so craftily planned
was suddenly no advantage at all. Those forted-up

Texans across the yard in Flying E's bunkhouse with their ready guns would very likely down both Burton and Ayers, but that wouldn't help either Doolin or Eagleton if Ayers was as fast and accurate as legend said he was, because they would both be dead.

Eagleton's nostrils flared as he expelled a big breath. "Mexican stand-off!" he exclaimed. "You'll get it the same time we do." He was addressing Mike Ayers. All that previous look of scorn was erased from his features now.

From a long way off came the fluting sound of a cowboy's call. This was answered closer in. After that came a deathless hush and Lew Burton, watching Doolin, saw Flying E's range boss shoot a look far out, roll his heavy brows together and slowly, infinitesimally swing his head from side to side. Lew smiled.

"Look yonder," breathed Doolin to Eagleton. "Riders comin' in from all around. Big mob of 'em, Cy."

But Eagleton didn't look; he was still watching Mike Ayers. There was a growing, reckless flame in the depths of his eyes. He was making an assessment many men before him had made, men of great confidence and strong arrogance. He was estimating his chances against a professional gunfighter and telling himself he was Ayers's match.

Mike knew it was coming with solid certainty. He stood there waiting, and, when he felt certain Eagleton was ready, he broke the cowman's intense concentration with one word.

"Draw!"

Doolin, still staring at the converging great number of incoming, surrounding horsemen, was unprepared until that one fierce word was snarled, then he tried to recover, tried to go for his gun, and jump clear at the same time.

Lew Burton, for several seconds now balancing atop his saddle lightly, flung himself sideward and downward. He hit the ground after those two explosions erupted with gray dust spurting upward from where he landed.

Ayers did not seem to have moved at all but black powder smoke engulfed his lower right side where a palmed six-gun reflected wicked sunlight.

Across the porch Cyrus Eagleton took one big staggering backward step, stopped with both shoulders against his house-front, with his fired gun drooping, and looked with purest astonishment at that gun in Mike Ayers's hand.

Eagleton's slug had gouged a raw hole in the verandah planking three feet in front of Mike Ayers. He had been struck hard a second before tugging off that shot.

Lefty Doolin sprang sideways toward the doorway at the same time, snapping off a shot at Lew Burton. He got inside a fraction ahead of Lew's answering shot.

Eagleton dropped his gun and slid down into a sitting position, his glazing eyes still fixed with disbelief upon the man who had shot him.

Mike's horse flung wildly away from those suddenly erupting lashes of crimson gun flame, whirled, and went careening back across the yard.

Doolin, inside the house, fired at Ayers through a window and the *tinkle* of broken glass was added to the other sounds.

Lew Burton whipped upright off the ground, got both legs under him, and hurtled ahead up onto the verandah, seeking to get against the house front where Doolin could not see him. Mike also launched himself forward, but he was thinking, not of Doolin inside the house, but of the gunfire that erupted now from down at the bunkhouse.

Bullets struck wood with a tearing sound. Another window exploded into a hundred fragments and Lew Burton loudly gasped. Mike, moving eastward, saw the sheriff arch his back, saw Lew's mouth fly wide open and his eyes turn frantic with sudden pain. He ran past Doolin's broken window, grabbed Lew with his free left hand, and wrenched him farther along. From behind that wrecked window Doolin fired again, but it was too late. Mike was furiously jerking Lew Burton toward the east end of Eagleton's house.

He made it, got around out of sight, and pushed the injured sheriff over against a sheltered house wall.

XVIII

That abrupt eruption of gunfire from the bunk-house brought another sound to Flying E's dusty yard as those converging, surrounding range riders joined the fight with loud shouts and a rattle of uneven gunfire.

Bullets whipped up dust before the bunkhouse, struck solidly against wooden siding, and shattered windows. For almost a full minute that bunkhouse was subjected to a terrific concentration of lead, and, as this eventually diminished, so did the return fire from Eagleton's Texans.

Around the side of Eagleton's house with the injured sheriff, Mike Ayers, for this little time, let the battle swirl on without him.

The bullet that had struck Lew Burton had evidently come from the bunkhouse. It had first struck a verandah upright that had flattened it, then it had, with diminished speed, struck Lew in the hip, laying open a wound resembling the broadside slash of a saber. Mike tore his neckerchief into a long strip for a bandage, staunched the spurting claret, told Lew to press his hand tightly over this makeshift dressing, and went to work creating a bandage out of the sheriff's shirt that would be large enough and strong enough to go completely around Burton where it could then be lashed down tightly enough to prevent additional bleeding.

This took a lot of time, but in Mike's view that

bleeding had to be stopped. Actually, although the hole in Burton's thigh was deep and ragged, this was not likely to prove a fatal injury, providing Lew did not lose too much blood. But it was a painful injury and Burton's lips, sucked flat, attested to his agony.

The gunfire started up again out in the yard, and now it was obvious that the posse men from Alturas had used that interlude of comparative quiet to work their way in among Flying E's outbuildings, for, as this steady firing increased, it was much louder and much closer.

Smoke drifted across the yard, dirty- and oily-looking, from all those attacking guns. There was the deep-throated roar of six-guns and the higher, sharper *crack* of carbines. From the bunkhouse the gunfire was almost entirely made by carbines.

Mike finished the bandaging and eased Lew back until his shoulders were against the house. He craned for a look at the bunkhouse, swung back, and looked at Lew.

"Go on," rumbled the sheriff. "I'll be all right. I'm just sorry I had to stop one. Damn that Doolin anyway."

Mike said nothing until he'd made another, close inspection of the sodden bandage to make certain the pressure had stopped that bleeding. "Don't worry about Doolin," he said, finally. "He's mine."

Mike got fully upright and glided southward on around the house to the back. He was confident Lew would be all right. There were no windows on the east side of Eagleton's house.

He made it around to the rear screened-in porch, got down low there, reached forth to pluck at the screen door, found it not only unlatched but easy to open, and, after a moment of careful listening, he scuttled on into what appeared to be a pantry, and stopped. From inside Eagleton's residence that outside gunfire sounded distant, sounded like a full-scale army attack.

He got through into Eagleton's kitchen, stood up next to a closed, intervening door, and listened. All that outside racket, though, effectively overrode any sounds inside the house. He stood there, assessing the situation and events that had brought him to where he now was, and concluded that Flying E was pinned down. Eagleton's Texans could not escape from their bunkhouse and Eagleton's range boss could not get out of the main ranch house.

All that remained, then, for the forces of the law to do was either wait them out or smoke them out. Waiting, he thought, might endanger John Arnold, and, like Lew Burton, Mike also believed the newspaperman was somewhere within the confines of Flying E's headquarters ranch.

A pistol shot exploded beyond Mike's kitchen door. This was the first shot Doolin had fired that Mike knew of, since the battle on the verandah. It placed Doolin for him, but it did not answer the paramount question of where John Arnold was.

Whomever Doolin had fired at out in the yard evidently had been not only missed, but had also been angered by that shot, because now, although Mike could not tell one of those numerous gunshots from another out there, he very distinctly heard bullets striking the front of the house.

For fully sixty seconds Doolin and that unknown posse man dueled back and forth. Mike tried counting Doolin's shots, thinking, when Doolin had emptied his six-gun, he might kick open the door and cover him. But, when Doolin had fired six slugs, he did not hesitate to reload, but continued firing. Doolin, Mike concluded, had more than one handgun with him, and that precluded for the time being anything as rash as Mike's plan of jumping past the door into the parlor.

There came a sudden lull in the outside firing again. Sporadic gunfire continued but the bulk of that deafening gun thunder atrophied. Mike cocked his head, listening; those range riders out there were up to something. When they'd slackened off before, it had been to creep down among Flying E's outbuildings.

Evidently Lefty Doolin also thought this, because he suddenly shouted a warning to the embattled Texans in the bunkhouse. Mike heard this outcry plainly, then he also heard something else, heard Doolin say something in an almost normal tone to someone else in the yonder parlor with him.

John Arnold! Without knowing how he knew who was in the other room with Doolin, Mike was certain it was Evelyn's father. He wondered, just for a second, what would have happened had he sprung through to face Doolin a moment before as he'd thought of doing, before he'd known Arnold was in there with Doolin.

A brisk rattle of gunfire broke out again in the yard. Mike listened, estimated that most of this was coming from behind the bunkhouse, and thought again that the posse men were up to something. Before, most of them had been facing that stout little building.

A man's bawling voice yelled something indistinguishable. Gunfire increased from the bunkhouse at this rumbling outcry and Mike frowned, wishing he dared cross to a window and peer out.

That bull-bass voice roared a second time. Other voices took up this indistinguishable yelling. Voices ringed the yard with their clamor and those embattled Texans forted-up out there stepped up their firing without answering those yells.

Mike smelled smoke and had his answer. The posse men had flanked Flying E's bunkhouse, had opened up all round it to drive its defenders from their windows, and had fired the building. He drew his handgun, cocked it, and waited. It could not be long now before this frantic fight ended. Without his allies at the burning bunkhouse Lefty Doolin would be finished.

That smell of smoke became stronger. In the yonder parlor Mike heard Doolin curse at his hostage, heard the hard sound of gun metal dragging over soft wood, and thought Doolin was moving clear of the front window, was probably far back in the parlor where he could safely stand up.

Men began shouting, their unmistakable Texas accents loudly resounding over the crackle of flames and the dying, ragged gunfire of the posse men. Flying E's rough Texas crew had had enough, they were shouting for quarter, their alternatives equally as grisly—burn to death or try and break out and be shot down in the exposed yard.

Mike brought up his gun hand. Whatever Lefty Doolin did, he must do very soon now, for with the surrender of his allies out in the yard, all that fierceness out there would be turned upon him.

Mike wondered if there was another back way out of Eagleton's house. There wasn't; he became

convinced of that almost the same second he thought
of it, because Doolin's rough voice came to him
clearly in the sudden hush, saying to someone beyond Mike's kitchen door: "Move out, damn you.
Stay in front of me and don't try to duck away or
run. Head for that kitchen door!"

Mike drew upright, hung there long enough to
hear a man's dragging steps, then eased steadily
back until, near the square opening leading out into
the pantry, he could fade out in a niche where gloom
lay in solid layers in front of a floor-to-ceiling cooler.
Here, unable to see around into the kitchen without
exposing himself, he raised his uncocked gun shoulder high, and waited. If Doolin was seeking to leave
the house by the rear exit, he and his hostage would
have to pass within eight inches of Mike's shadowy
place of concealment.

Catcalls erupted out in the yard made by men
whose hooting exultation indicated Flying E's tough
Texans were emerging from the burning bunkhouse, hands high over their heads. Mike heard those
two, Doolin and Arnold, pass on into the kitchen,
pause, evidently to gauge the reason for all that cat-
calling out front, then start toward him.

"Remember," Flying E's range boss said again,
"don't get more'n five feet ahead of me, Arnold, and,
if you make one bad move . . . you're dead!"

It was a bad moment for Mike Ayers. His timing
would have to be perfect; otherwise, Doolin might
see him or sight movement, and fire. If that happened, he would be too close to either Arnold or Ayers to miss. There was a simple way out for Mike but
he chose not to take it and continued there, standing
rigidly with that upraised gun ready, hoping to catch
Doolin across the skull before he himself were seen.

It didn't work out that way. As John Arnold stepped through the pantry doorway, he instinctively looked to his left, into that dingy place where Mike was waiting, and Arnold's breath snagged in his throat, his stride faltered at sight of Ayers where he'd expected to see no one, and both of these indications of shocked surprise were instant warnings to Lefty Doolin.

Mike, his high hopes shattered, had to move now and move fast. He did. He lunged forward, striking at John Arnold with his left hand, dropping his right hand at the same time Doolin fired.

That violent explosion sounded twice as loud within the confines of Eagleton's pantry. The bullet struck wood beside the screen door inches from where Arnold had been before Mike slammed him out of the way.

Doolin let off a wild bellow, jumped back, and swung for another shot. Mike dropped flat down, snapped off an upward shot, and frantically rolled sideways. He was inside the kitchen past the pantry door when he did this, which saved him from Doolin's second bullet. That one ripped a long, thin splinter out of the cooler, burying itself deeply into soft pine wood.

Mike's bullet caught Doolin high in the body, half turned him, and Doolin's third shot went straight down through the floor at his feet. Mike stopped rolling, brought his six-gun to bear, and fired. Doolin went crashing drunkenly over into a table, broke it with his fall, and lay utterly still amid the wreckage of that table. After that silence returned.

Mike got up stiffly, slowly dusted himself off, crossed over to peer down at dead Lefty Doolin, kicked Doolin's gun away, turned, and peered out where John Arnold lay flat upon the pantry floor. He started for the newspaperman, then halted and methodically reloaded his six-gun before continuing forward.

Several men came soft-footing it around the house. One of them called ahead, saying Mike's name, saying it was all over outside and wanting to know if help was needed inside. Mike listened but did not reply to this call; instead, he went out to John Arnold, knelt and rolled Arnold over, looking for the location of Arnold's wound. When he found no bullet puncture, no blood, not even any torn clothing, he holstered his gun, called for the outside cowboys to come in, and stood up again.

When the cattlemen crowded in, some straining around Ayers to peer in where Doolin lay sprawled, some gazing straight down at Arnold's sprawled form, Ayers said dryly: "Doolin's finished. Arnold here . . . you can fetch a bucket of water and toss it over him. He fainted."

Mike stepped over John Arnold, shouldered through the gaping posse men, pushed on outside, and hiked back around where Lew Burton was being looked after by at least ten men. He edged his way in, eased down beside Lew, and thumbed back his hat.

"How're you feelin'?" he asked.

"The best I've felt in years," retorted the sheriff. "They got what's left of Eagleton's salty Texas crew lined up out there in the yard." Lew paused, ran a quick, rummaging glance over Mike's face, and said: "Was John in there?"

Mike nodded. "Yeah. He's all right. He fainted when Doolin and I shot it out."

"You all right, Mike?"

"Fit as a fiddle, but I could use a drink."

The cowmen, standing around listening, chuckled and responded to this with comments of their own. Mike looked up at them, half smiling. "On me," he said, "when we get back to Alturas. Right now, couple of you rustle up a wagon for the sheriff and let's head back for town." He stood up as the cowmen began moving off, looked down at Lew, and solemnly winked. Just as solemnly, Lew winked back.

About the Author

Lauran Paine who, under his own name and various pseudonyms has written over 1,000 books, was born in Duluth, Minnesota. His family moved to California when he was at a young age and his apprenticeship as a Western writer came about through the years he spent in the livestock trade, rodeos, and even motion pictures where he served as an extra because of his expert horsemanship. He served in the U.S. Navy in the Second World War. Paine's Western fiction is characterized by strong plots, authenticity, an apparently effortless ability to construct situation and character, and a preference for building his stories upon a solid foundation of historical fact.

INTERACT WITH DORCHESTER ONLINE!

Want to learn more about your favorite
books and authors?
Want to talk with other readers that like
to read the same books as you?
Want to see up-to-the-minute Dorchester
news?

VISIT DORCHESTER AT:
DorchesterPub.com
Twitter.com/DorchesterPub
Facebook.com (Search Pages)

DISCUSS DORCHESTER'S NOVELS AT:
Dorchester Forums at DorchesterPub.com
GoodReads.com
LibraryThing.com
Myspace.com/books
Shelfari.com
WeRead.com

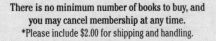

☐ **YES!**

Sign me up for the Leisure Western Book Club and send my FREE BOOKS! If I choose to stay in the club, I will pay only $14.00* each month, a savings of $9.96!

NAME: _____

ADDRESS: _____

TELEPHONE: _____

EMAIL: _____

☐ I want to pay by credit card.

☐ VISA   ☐ MasterCard   ☐ DISCOVER

ACCOUNT #: _____

EXPIRATION DATE: _____

SIGNATURE: _____

Mail this page along with $2.00 shipping and handling to:
Leisure Western Book Club
PO Box 6640
Wayne, PA 19087
Or fax (must include credit card information) to:
610-995-9274

You can also sign up online at **www.dorchesterpub.com**.
*Plus $2.00 for shipping. Offer open to residents of the U.S. and Canada only.
Canadian residents please call 1-800-481-9191 for pricing information.
If under 18, a parent or guardian must sign. Terms, prices and conditions subject to change. Subscription subject to acceptance. Dorchester Publishing reserves the right to reject any order or cancel any subscription.